BINKY AND DOAN'S MEDITATIONS
ON DETECTING

"Ahh, sweet money!" Bink[...]

"Think of it," Doan said, r[...]
buy the full line of Aveda hair [...]

"Unlimited M.A.C. cosmetic[...]

"Wodehouse first editions."

"Armani sunglasses."

"Armani *socks*!"

"Chauffeurs."

"Fresh cut flowers all the time."

"Not just daisies—tulips! irises! weird tropical-looking thingies!"

"Ahhh," they chorused together.

Praise for
DEATH WORE A SMART LITTLE OUTFIT

MORE MYSTERIES FROM THE
BERKLEY PUBLISHING GROUP ...

DOAN AND BINKY MYSTERIES: San Francisco's dazzling detective team is back and better than ever. These detectives have a fashion sense to *die* for ... "An entertaining cozy with a nineties difference."—*MLB News*

by Orland Outland
DEATH WORE A SMART LITTLE OUTFIT   DEATH WORE A FABULOUS NEW FRAGRANCE

DOG LOVERS' MYSTERIES STARRING JACKIE WALSH: She's starting a new life with her son and an ex-police dog named Jake ... teaching film classes and solving crimes!

by Melissa Cleary
A TAIL OF TWO MURDERS
DOG COLLAR CRIME
HOUNDED TO DEATH
FIRST PEDIGREE MURDER
SKULL AND DOG BONES

DEAD AND BURIED
THE MALTESE PUPPY
MURDER MOST BEASTLY
OLD DOGS

SAMANTHA HOLT MYSTERIES: Dogs, cats, and crooks are all part of a day's work for this veterinary technician ... "Delightful!"—Melissa Cleary

by Karen Ann Wilson
EIGHT DOGS FLYING
BEWARE SLEEPING DOGS

COPY CAT CRIMES
CIRCLE OF WOLVES

CHARLOTTE GRAHAM MYSTERIES: She's an actress with a flair for dramatics—and an eye for detection. "You'll get hooked on Charlotte Graham!"—*Rave Reviews*

by Stefanie Matteson
MURDER AT THE SPA
MURDER AT TEATIME
MURDER ON THE CLIFF
MURDER ON THE SILK ROAD

MURDER AT THE FALLS
MURDER ON HIGH
MURDER AMONG THE ANGELS
MURDER UNDER THE PALMS

PEACHES DANN MYSTERIES: Peaches has never had a very good memory. But she's learned to cope with it over the years ... Fortunately, though, when it comes to murder, this absentminded amateur sleuth doesn't forgive and forget!

by Elizabeth Daniels Squire
WHO KILLED WHAT'S-HER-NAME?
MEMORY CAN BE MURDER
REMEMBER THE ALIBI

WHOSE DEATH IS IT, ANYWAY?
IS THERE A DEAD MAN IN THE HOUSE?

HEMLOCK FALLS MYSTERIES: The Quilliam sisters combine their culinary and business skills to run an inn in upstate New York. But when it comes to murder, their talent for detection takes over ...

by Claudia Bishop
A TASTE FOR MURDER
A PINCH OF POISON
A DASH OF DEATH

MURDER WELL-DONE
DEATH DINES OUT

DEATH WORE A

Fabulous

NEW FRAGRANCE

❦

Orland Outland

BERKLEY PRIME CRIME, NEW YORK

DEATH WORE A FABULOUS NEW FRAGRANCE

A Berkley Prime Crime Book / published by arrangement with the author

PRINTING HISTORY
Berkley Prime Crime edition / June 1998

The Penguin Putnam Inc. World Wide Web site address is
http://www.penguinputnam.com

ISBN: 0-425-16197-8

PRINTED IN THE UNITED STATES OF AMERICA

10 9 8 7 6 5 4 3 2 1

DEATH WORE A

Fabulous

NEW FRAGRANCE

ONE

$\mathcal{B}$inky had her shoes off before the front door of her building had closed behind her. At that moment, there was no doubt in her mind that any job, even one cleaning toilets, would be superior to *looking* for a job; no doubt that nothing any maid could ever see in any hotel room could be more depressing than filling out a dozen applications in one day.

"That information is all on my resume," she'd told the morning's first receptionist, handing back the blank application. She had filled out a dozen the day before, and had consequently borrowed her friend KC's talents that night to computerize and print out a resume so as to be prepared today.

"Yes," the receptionist said, "but they want you to fill out an application anyway." So she had laboriously copied everything off the resume and onto the application. Then she had been ushered into the presence of a personnel officer, who read all the information on her application, said "Hmm," read it all over again on her resume, then smiled and told her that the position had been filled earlier that day, but that they would certainly keep her application on file. This scenario, with slight variations, had been repeated everywhere she went.

She didn't really want a job and, to tell the truth, didn't really need one. A trust fund set up before she was even born provided enough money to take care of her daily needs, or at least what her trustees considered daily needs. Things she thought fell into that category, like Jamaica Blue Mountain coffee, Perrier-Jouët, silk lingerie, weekly hairdressing, taxicabs, shrimp salad, chocolate truffles, and the like, she was cruelly expected to provide for herself. She'd quit her last job on the spur of the moment, when her friend Doan had called her with the irresistible offer of a week in Bermuda with himself and, not incidentally, Luke, the most gorgeous man in the universe. Then she'd gotten caught up in international intrigue, theft, murder, and kidnapping. However, once the bad were punished, that was the end of it. Someone had forgotten to include the part about the good being rewarded. Well, she had gotten Luke. But then she had gotten rid of Luke, to the consternation of everyone who'd ever known him . . . hell, who'd ever *seen* him. That whole drama, she thought, was far too complicated to be thought of as any kind of real reward.

Anyway, she was unemployed, and bored as well, thanks to a serious lack of spending money. Lacking the ability to shop, she told herself that since she didn't have anything to do during the day, since she didn't much care for going out alone, and since Doan was hardly speaking to her since she'd dumped Luke, she might as well go back to work.

She wasn't exactly going about her search in a methodical and diligent way. Having spent six months typing reports for the police department, this time she was intent on finding a line of work that was, if not at least a little more exciting, then at least a little better paying. Consequently she spent her days applying for jobs like Administrative Assistant to the President, Executive Secretary, Assistant Director. The fact that she had absolutely no experience in any of these fields made no difference to her. She was smart, she was pretty, she could learn. She felt sure that the captains of industry, those great men who had made their companies what they were today, would agree with her. The problem was that she could never get past their narrow-minded, convention-bound personnel officers.

She trudged up the stairs to her apartment with her mail, flipping through it as she went: two bills, which she added to the pile already overflowing the basket next to the door, and a letter from her family back East. This, sure to be another indignity in a day full of them, she threw onto the kitchen table for later. She popped open a pony bottle of Korbel (her weak stab at economy), fell on the couch with a dramatic groan, and reached for the phone. Doan had warmed noticeably to her these last few days, his hatred of jobs and job hunting causing him to be momentarily sympathetic, even to the point of forgetting how upset he was at her for dropping Luke.

Doan answered on the first ring. "Yeah?"

"Me."

"Hi."

The general mirthlessness of this exchange demoralized both of them even further. "I've been job hunting," Binky said. "What's your excuse?"

"Just got through moving out of his place. I was sure I'd be done before he got home, but it was not to be." Like Binky, Doan had gotten drunk on the heady vapors of adventure, and had found romance with a man about as capable of living with Doan as Dick was with Liz. KC was, to put it mildly, a bit more domestically inclined than Doan. For the sake of true love, Doan, who had lived most of his adult life in dresses, had put on pants, worked one job eight hours a day, stayed home on Friday and Saturday nights, and entertained KC's friends on Sunday afternoons. At the end of one month, he had run quite literally screaming out of KC's house, not to be seen again for three days. At the end of that time he presented himself on Binky's doorstep, back in a dress, back to holding five part-time jobs, back in his own posh Pacific Heights apartment (paid for by a former beau), and back to his assertion that one should only marry out of dire economic necessity.

"Oh, honey! Was there a horrible scene?"

"Worse. Just those long, silent looks of recrimination and pain. I was simply not cut out to live in a Bergman film, thank you. I am, consequently, currently eating my way through an entire pint of double chocolate fudge chocolate chip chocolate chunk ice cream. Mmm, mmm!" he stated defiantly. "Did I forget to tell you that another of his little foibles is that he's a health nut? Carob once a week, he quite strongly suggested, would be more satisfying than chocolate whenever the need hits."

Binky loved KC dearly, but this was clearly an indefensible position to take.

"And no pastry. Ever. Champagne? Far too expensive. We are mature responsible adults saving our money for a house and our retirement."

"I've got a pony open here," she offered, half to console him, half to lure him over to console her.

"I'm calling a cab as we speak," he said, hanging up.

The problem with a pony, Binky and Doan quickly realized, is that it is so very small. This, they decided, was a time of crisis in their lives, and consequently it was impossible to economize. In a rather frenzied few minutes, they talked themselves out of the apartment and down to a posh restaurant, where they allowed their waiter to pour from a seemingly bottomless magnum. After crab-stuffed mushroom caps, Oysters Rockefeller, Coquilles St. Jacques, and strawberries in cream, they felt a little less like victims.

"How will we pay for this?" she asked.

"Oh, I'll just charge it."

"What will you do when the bill comes?"

"That's not for another month. By which time, I will have found a wealthy man to marry. Maybe a doctor, definitely a workaholic, so I can have the place to myself most of the time. You and I will go to the Virgin Islands, or somewhere like that, and take lovers."

Binky sighed. It sounded wonderful. "I wish I could find a young, attractive, charming, intelligent, and witty man, who also just happens to be rich."

"Sorry. There are three of those, at last count. Two met and married each other, the other was last seen six months ago scaling Mt. Everest. Of course, if you were willing to just forget the rich part . . ." he trailed off.

She glowered at him. "Luke and I are over. I wish you'd see that, and let it alone."

"Sorry, simply can't. Especially since you still haven't explained your actions to my satisfaction."

She shook her head. She always found herself groping for words when she thought about Luke. She thought she'd come upon part of the solution, when she'd remembered him staring at her in the darkened bedroom as she came back from the bathroom, and staring at her in the kitchen as she'd made coffee. She was, quite simply, frightened of so much love. But to say it out loud—somehow, it didn't sound like a credible reason for an adult to give for breaking off an affair. Loving someone back that much meant the end of something; she wasn't sure what, but it was something she wasn't ready to let go of.

"What about you and KC?" she diverted him.

"That was different," he said brusquely, tossing back his coffee and throwing his Visa card on top of the check. "Luke did not expect you to entertain people you would never in a million years have otherwise met socially. Luke did not expect you to tolerate friendly pats on the ass in accompaniment to requests for more beer and chips for 'the boys' during their Sunday afternoon football fest. Luke did not blink blankly at any reference to any motion picture made before 1960. Luke did not expect you to do all the housework and look up to him as your savior from a wasted life. *Luke did not look up from the sautéed scallops you had prepared for him with your own fair hand and tell you he was a meat and potatoes kind of guy himself!*'' The waiter had returned with his card; Doan signed the receipt quickly. ''Shall we?'' he asked, throwing his napkin down and getting up. They walked out into the chilly night air.

''I'll make a deal with you,'' Binky offered. ''You stop bugging me about Luke, at least until this job-hunting nightmare is over, and I won't bug you about KC.''

''Deal. Oh, honey, I'm sorry,'' Doan said, wrapping his arm around her. ''Life is hard enough without the two of us, of all people, fighting over anything.'' He sighed. ''You know, with all the notoriety we got after saving Eleanor and catching Charles and Alholm, I was sure there was going to be some money in there some-place.''

Binky thought back on those days of celebrity. Were they really only a month ago? Their intrepid gang had been all over the papers as the nabbers of the SoMa Killer. It was, in her eyes, the crime of the century. She felt sure that, in a day and age when having too many traffic tickets was good enough to get a TV-movie made about your life, the offers for their story would come rolling in. This was partially why she'd delayed her job hunt for so long—how could she be away from home when Hollywood would be ringing her phone with movie offers, when New York would be calling with a bid for the story written in her own words?

She had completely forgotten that there were, after all, an inordinate number of homosexuals involved in the story, none of whom died as a result of this vile sin. Not to mention the presence of Doan, of whom it could safely be said that no amount of toning down would render him suitable for the multiplex.

"Although . . ." he said casually, and Binky knew something was up.

"Spit it out, Doan."

"I was just thinking, that's all. Even though nobody wants to pay us for our story, I think we can still capitalize on this. After all, we're still recognized on the street here, people know we're famous crime stoppers. Right?"

"What on earth is all this leading up to?"

"Why, my dear, it's simple. We open a detective agency!"

She kept a straight face for a full half-second before bursting into laughter. "Come off it!"

"What?" he demanded. "It's a good idea!"

"Doan, please. In the first place, it's a business. A business needs money to start. Which neither of us has. And getting a loan is out of the question, when you have no collateral."

"What about your trust fund?"

"It's locked up six ways to nowhere. Not usable for loan purposes. And a detective's license! You have to have some kind of experience to get one, I'm sure. And do you really think we'd get any customers? Why are you smiling?"

"You've already thought about this, haven't you?"

They burst out laughing together. "Of course I have. I've considered everything except—no, *including*—selling my body in order to get out of having to go back to work in an office. But that was just a foolish fantasy."

"No, it's not. Look here. We get an office the same way anyone with no money gets an office—we sign a lease for a million years, because the longer the lease, the lower your rent. We can get into one of those great old buildings on Market for a song."

"What happens if we go bust, and we have this lease?"

He shrugged. "If the company goes bust, then we're broke. How are they going to make us pay? What are they going to take from us? Our good looks?"

"Customers. We'd never get customers."

"Eleanor will take care of that," he replied, mentioning the famous socialite they had rescued from the clutches of her evil husband. "She'll get all her rich friends to hire us. All they spend their money on is lunch, their hair, and detectives to follow their husbands. You know what I never understood? Why a woman would spend such a staggering amount of money to make her hair look just like a cheap wig! And as to lunch, how can they spend so much on that when they don't eat a thing, ever?!"

"Doan," she said, cutting him off.

"Sorry."

"And the license, Doan."

"Oh, I have a friend downtown, who we've agreed not to discuss."

"That tears it. No way!" She stormed ahead of him.

"What?"

"I will not be indebted to Luke Faraglione!"

"Of course you won't. I will." He caught up with her. "Did I tell you he's just been promoted? The world of officialdom is his oyster!"

"No."

He jumped in front of her and blocked her way. There was a serious gleam in his eye that made her stop. "Then listen to this. You've been screwing around with this job thing, and you know it. As it stands now, you've got three options. One, you can do without all the things that make life worth living. Or two, you can get another hideous job that will depress you. Or you can become a real detective. Make your own hours, be your own boss!"

"You're sounding like a matchbook cover."

"Well, it's true. And what's more, I'm going to do it."

They walked together in silence for a while, until they found themselves in the shopping district, in front of Tiffany's as the display cases were being emptied for the night. Looking at all the beautiful things, watching them being snatched from her gaze, Binky felt sure that she was being sent a message.

"Okay."

"Do you mean it?"

"If you're going to do it anyways, I might as well join you."

"*Yippee!*" Doan screamed, and Binky laughed.

"We're going to get in a hell of a lot of trouble when this falls through, you know."

"It won't. Trust me!"

The next day, Doan met Luke for lunch at a charming little sidewalk cafe on Polk Street, which it would do no good to name as it changes hands between the time you are handed the menu and the time you are handed the bill. Even on this street, as close as San Francisco gets to having a Boulevard of Broken Dreams, where male prostitutes, punk rockers, drag queens, and assorted odd lots mix, the sight of the tall slender man in the dress at the table with the well-built, six-foot-four, black-haired, blue-eyed, olive-skinned—well, *perfect*—man was enough to turn heads.

"So what did she say?" Luke asked in greeting, stretching languidly as if to belie his interest in the answer. "Did she agree?"

Doan watched the frame expand and contract and sat down, overcome, before answering. "Yes, eventually. Nothing like a vision of another typing pool to put the fear of God into the girl. Mind you, she's sure failure is just around the corner. And, of course, she wants to make sure that we all understand that I am indebted to you and she is not.''

Luke shrugged and smiled his killer smile, as lazy as his stretch. Doan envied him his confidence. As far as Luke was concerned, he had found his dream girl in Binky, and dreams were always difficult to fulfill. She would come around sooner or later, he was sure.

''I even told her you got promoted.''

''What did she say to that?''

''She didn't seem to be paying attention.'' Noticing Luke's slightly hurt look, he hastened to add, ''In particular. Actually, the mere mention of you throws her into a general panic.''

''She wouldn't do that if she wasn't still fond of me, would she?'' he asked rhetorically, sure of the answer.

''No. As if anyone could stop being fond of you, dear. Now the trick is for us to get involved in some crime or another, and have to call you in on it. The two of you working in such close proximity on a matter of such importance . . . well, need I say more? Although my personal experience,'' he said drily, ''with combining romance and adventure is not a pleasant memory, I think, quite frankly, that she could be tantalized by a little adventure right now. She really wasn't as involved as the rest of us were in the SoMa Killer case.''

Luke laughed. '' 'Case'? You're sounding like a detective already.''

''Feeling like one is the first step to being one. At least in my book. So, how's the permit going?''

''Oh, that.'' Luke reached into his jacket and produced an envelope. ''Here you go.''

''Is it . . .'' He took the envelope with trepidation, then opened it. ''Oh my god, I'm a detective!'' He jumped up, ran around the table, and hugged Luke for all he was worth. ''Oh, I knew you'd come through!''

"Just be careful. Because you don't have any experience working for either a law enforcement agency or a detective agency, you're on a year's probation. As far as the State Board is concerned, the SoMa Killer was caught by good police work."

"That's true. No one could have done it but you."

"Doan, you're the one who did it."

"True. But what other cop but you would have had the sense to let me handle it?"

Luke laughed. "No one."

Doan got up. "I'd love to stay, but I just remembered my produce store is closing early today, and if I don't get there in time, my culinary plans for the weekend are ruined. Thank you again, love. And you know I won't rest until justice is done."

"The criminals are cowering already."

"Huh? Oh, that. But I meant the more important matter—namely, you and Binky. Bye!"

For Binky, the future was an amorphous concept. Planning for it, preparing for it, laying the groundwork for it were alien notions to her. Of course, she was not alone in this, especially in San Francisco. Informal polling and ill-informed prejudice clearly show that our fair city has a larger number of trust fund babies loitering away their lives than any other city. (Should you care, real, actual, boring statistics support this by asserting that San Francisco does have the highest per capita income in the U.S.) With $30,000 a year coming to her from her trust fund, Binky had enough—more than enough, really, for a sensible, frugal girl; the problem was that she was neither of those things. Only in a town so rich could the *San Francisco Chronicle* run an article about, gee, how hard it is to live on $100,000 a year—after all, there's the Jaguar to pay for, the second house, the private school—hey, man, it's a real struggle. Doan had become apoplectic on reading this article; Binky thought it was the truest thing that rag had ever printed.

When the future looked bleak, Binky lost whatever shred of interest she might have had in planning for it. But now the future, while, frankly, still looking bleak— she had complete adoration for Doan and absolutely no faith in him as a businessman—was at least planned out for her. In a few weeks, Doan would have secured an office, a phone, probably even a secretary. She did not underestimate his talent for logistics, only his willingness to stick with something after it got boring (a dilemma she understood too well).

But, she reminded herself, it would be fun while it lasted. And since the pressure to get a real job was off her, and since she had a couple of weeks to kill before going into the detective business, work suddenly seemed like an amusing lark, being as it was something she'd only have to do for two weeks. Get out! Meet people! See the world! (More likely, see a fluorescent-lit office with no windows, but she put that to the side in a rare burst of enthusiasm.)

So she signed up at last with a temp agency that had offered her menial work before, which she'd been too good to accept. Now that she was about to go into business, of course, the agency immediately became interested in her. "Can you start tomorrow?" asked Amy, the perky agency rep.

"What's the job?" she asked, not much caring but enjoying her power to refuse just about anything.

Amy leaned over to whisper a state secret. "I'm sure you know Jeff Breeze."

"I'm sure I don't," she replied—a falsehood, of sorts: it was impossible to read the sort of fluffy magazines Binky read and not be subjected to numerous profiles of movie stars; nonetheless, she did not "know" Jeff Breeze, and so in her mind, this was not a lie.

Amy was at a loss. "The movie star?"

"Has he been dead more than twenty years?"

"No!" She laughed.

"Then I am unacquainted with him."

Amy, mistaking Binky for a girl who could relate, sighed and tilted her head to one side. "He's soooo cute. He's hunky, he's good looking, he's a family man. . . ." Seeing that Binky had unsubtly begun inspecting her nails, Amy got down to business. "He's going to be at Macy's tomorrow, launching his new fragrance, called Closer. They need people to spray the testers and hand out samples. And you may even get to meet Jeff!" She leaned in closer. "Listen. I'll give you the job, if you'll just get this signed for me." She handed Binky an issue of *People* with Jeff Breeze and his lovely wife on the cover.

"Oh, joy. I'll take it."

"He's a big queen!" Doan shouted indignantly, after Binky had recapped Amy's description of the movie star for Doan. A bottle of Jouet had been required to celebrate her employment. Neither side spoiled the chance to drink bubbly by reminding themselves or each other that the cost of the bottle was more than she would make at work tomorrow.

"How do you know?"

"It's just one of those things every gay man knows. How to accessorize, how to get by on your looks, and how to tell which movie stars are gay. Didn't you hear about the summer he spent on Fire Island when he was practically a kid? He'd just done his first movie, some teen cum extravaganza, and Randall Reid had him at his house on the island for three months! And honey, that's not a gig you get without putting out. And then there's the weekend he spent in Hawaii with Matthew Brady—"

"But he's married," she protested. Seeing Doan's look of pity, she added, "They've got kids. . . ."

"Adopted," he emphasized. "Jeff Breeze is gay. Gay, gay, gay. But nobody will ever write the truth."

"Why not?"

Doan sighed. "Listen, since you'll be at Macy's tomorrow spritzing the hapless mobs, Kenny Wells is sure to be there. He's the gay community's resident detector of Hollywood homophobia. Haven't you ever seen his column in the *Watchtower*?" The *Watchtower* in question was not that esteemed Jehovah's Witness publication, but rather one of San Francisco's many gay papers. It was not unreasonable to think that Binky might have read it, seeing as how it lay on the coffee tables of all her gay friends.

"Oh, I think so. It's always the third page of the Arts section, isn't it?"

"The first inside page, Kenny says. The inside front cover is always an ad, and that doesn't count—at least, not when you're trying to make your literary reputation."

"What kind of a reputation do you get writing for a gay rag?"

"You'd be amazed at the fabulous heights some— okay, very few, but some—people have scaled to after rising from the mire of the gay press. At any rate," Doan huffed, "Kenny will be there protesting."

"Protesting what? To save the whales from being turned into Jeff Breeze's cologne?"

"No, to out Jeff Breeze. It's the perfect opportunity. Lots of people, lots of press—*Entertainment Tonight, E!, Hard Copy*—everybody who matters. He's going to spray Breeze with Closer as he denounces him as a closet case, on national TV!"

Binky thought this sounded rather entertaining, and said so.

"That it might be," Doan agreed. "But if there's not blood on the walls before tomorrow is over, I don't know San Francisco!"

TWO

$\mathcal{B}$inky's amusement at working for a day was cut short before she began. The crowd outside Macy's was, in a word, unreal. More people had showed up to see an actor in the flesh than had gathered to see the future Emperor of Japan and his wife, "and almost," the breathless queen inside the store told her, "as many people as showed up to see *Liz!*" The consequence of this excitement was, first and foremost, too many people for Binky's taste, especially after she'd had to force her way through all of them to get to the store's employee entrance.

"Remember," the brisk, bun-headed rep from the cologne company that made Closer had told Binky and her fellow willowy, aristocratic-looking testers, "ask before you spray. If you don't you might get hurt, and that won't be our legal responsibility. When men ask you out or ask for your phone number, tell them it's company policy that we don't date customers. If they tell you they know it's not Macy's policy, tell them you work for the perfume company." The other girls treated this much as a frequent flyer would the preflight safety instructions. Binky seemed to be the only one who hadn't been here before. Bored, she tried to strike up a conversation with the woman next to her.

"This is my first time doing this," she admitted, hoping candid innocence would break the woman's frosty demeanor.

"I'm only doing this because my girlfriend needs money for school," she complained. "The pay sucks, but it's only for a day, and we get paid cash at the end."

"Cash? I didn't think temp agencies did that."

Artfully sculpted eyebrows were raised. "Oh, you're through the agency. You should have just called the publicist; they're the ones who pay cash."

"How much, if I can ask?" Binky asked through gritted teeth, extracting Amy's copy of *People* from her purse, dropping it onto the floor, and grinding it beneath her heel.

"Twenty bucks an hour. About what they're paying the temp agency. Who, of course, doesn't pay you even close to that. My girlfriend's right—capitalism sucks!"

Although she had just been put into no mood to argue, Binky thought that it had probably taken a hell of a lot of capitalism to pay for this chick's teeth to be so well capped. Ten bucks an hour, she thought indignantly, with taxes taken out, when she could have had twenty free and clear!

"Try and get as many people as possible to take the sample," the perfume company rep continued. "It's got Jeff's picture on the wrapper, so your main problem will be people asking for more than one. One per customer is our limit." Binky looked over at a pallet stacked high with boxes of samples, and figured that even the crush of fools outside couldn't exhaust this supply. She mentioned this to Frosty, who shrugged. "Of course they want the rubes to think there's a limited supply, so they'll want it more. 'The aura of exclusivity can transform a hum-drum product into a necessity.'"

"Marx?" Binky hazarded an ill-informed guess.

"My girlfriend's thesis. 'Shopping and Denial in Postindustrial America.' Have you got a cigarette?" This at last produced a topic that made Binky comfortable. She did indeed have a cigarette, and the two of them took advantage of being in the back of the crowd to worm away to the smokers' lounge, where Frosty introduced herself as Eliza.

"So are you here because you're a Jeff Breeze fan?" Eliza asked her.

"No, not me. I need the money."

"Thank God. I mean, I'd still be nice to you because you gave me a smoke, but I'd have to hate you."

"Because Jeff Breeze is gay, and I'd be a fool to be mad for him?" she asked, feeling a little better-informed on this subject.

"That, plus the guy's a drip. My girlfriend didn't want me to take this gig, she said it would make me a tool of heterocentrist oppression. I said, if the heterocentrist oppressor wants to give me twenty bucks an hour, why shouldn't I snatch the cash right out of his hands?"

"Amen to that," Binky agreed.

"Besides, I told her I'd give her the full report, and she could use this as a case study in her thesis. We'd better get back," Eliza said, having smoked an entire cigarette in four drags.

On their return, they found the other girls lined up to receive a basket full of sample vials and a tester. Eliza discreetly pulled a small cassette recorder out of her pocket. "Straw basket," she noted. "Typical and becoming feminine accessory in the minds of the patriarchy." It *was* becoming, Binky noted, making plans to steal her own (and maybe Eliza's) and take it home.

"All right, everybody," the rep said. "Jeff will be here in half an hour. When those people see you, they'll know he's coming. I want you to act like runway models! Come down that ramp and work it!''

While Binky knew little about modeling, she did know how to work it, and affected her best "screw you" look as she and the other hapless tools of patriarchy slunk down into the mob on the ramp that had been built from the delivery entrance.

"Jeff! Jeff!'' a woman began screaming, before fainting dead away. She was promptly crushed by others shouting "Where?'' From her lofty perch, Binky estimated the crowd to be about half young women and half gay men. At the back of the crowd, she could see signs waving feebly. '' 'Closer'?'' one sign asked, "or 'Closet'?'' Flipped around, it read, "Don't get any Closer.'' This was plainly Doan's friend Kenny and his contingent, well shoved away from the center of attention by excellent security.

"Free sample?'' she asked once before the mob descended on her. "Jeff! Jeff!'' the beast roared. Only later would she discover that this was the first look the villagers had had at the cologne's packaging, reproduced on the card that held the sample vial. "Oh my god, he's so beautiful,'' one man swooned, grasping his sample, which had a sepia-toned reproduction of a Bruce Weber photo of Breeze, face upturned, cheekbones boldly slicing the future. It looked like an outtake from a Lina Wertmuller film.

Her basket was emptied in seconds, then snatched out of her hand. "Hey! That's my souvenir!'' she protested. Clutching the spray tester, her last official emblem, she figured there was no returning for more samples, so she made her way toward the waving signs, where she found Doan and, presumably, Kenny, who was arguing with a police officer.

"I have a right to protest! I don't need a permit!'' Kenny was short, pale, and thin, with a buzz cut, a wispy goatee, and little round glasses. It was a popular urban look; it said "I'm an intellectual" to strangers without one's having to actually discuss ideas in order to prove it.

"Macy's has asked us to ask you to leave," the cop said, clearly more interested in the cute girls screaming for Jeff than in the half-dozen protesters who were bound to get no closer to their target (teenage girls who are in love with you are a far more efficient defense force than any number of toughs).

"Well, I'm not going to. Jeff Breeze is G-A-Y gay, and I want the world to know it! Closer stinks!" he shouted, for the benefit of TV cameras that were as likely to hear and see him as he was to hear and see Breeze.

"Hey," Binky said, recognizing the cop both as a pal of Luke's and as an acquaintance of her own from her days typing reports for the police department.

"Hey, Binky," Chuck said. "Are these friends of yours?"

Kenny, looking at her, nodded once. Binky nodded back. "Nodding acquaintances," she said truthfully.

"Too bad about you and Luke. You know, if it was anything he did, he regrets it. He looks terrible these days. If you two could patch it up . . ."

"See!" Doan crowed. "Everybody wants you back together. Who are you to resist the will of the majority?"

"No, Chuck, we won't be patching it up."

"Can I tell him you said hi?"

"No."

He departed, having discharged his duties to both Luke and Macy's, albeit unsuccessfully in both cases. "These beasts stole my basket," Binky said, indicating the many-headed monster.

"So many gay men here," Doan said, looking around. "Don't they have jobs?"

"They snuck out of their comfortable downtown of-fices," Kenny complained bitterly, "from the jobs that

a generation of gay activists worked to get for them, to
see a gay man who lives a lie and who helps keep gay
men around the country—around the world!—living a
lie.''

''I'm sorry,'' Doan said, taking Binky's arm. ''I know
the ill effect serious ideas have on you. Oh, is that the
tester? Can I have it?''

''Doan!'' Both Kenny and Binky reproved him.

''Not for use,'' he said scornfully. ''It'll be worth a
lot of money to one of these queens, and why shouldn't
I, an out gay man, take some of the money off their
hands they would otherwise give to a closeted gay
man?''

''Have you met Eliza?'' Binky asked.

''Who?''

''Never mind. No, you may not have the tester. I need
to turn it back in to get paid. What's so special about it
anyway?''

Doan rolled his eyes. He took it from her hands and
turned it sideways, so she could see Breeze's distinct
profile chiseled in the side of the bottle. ''And just think,
most gay men only get their penises cast in immortal
form!''

''Well,'' said a new voice. ''I should have known I'd
find you here.''

''I should have known I'd find you here, you . . . you
Stepin Fetchit! You parasite! I suppose you're here to
see Jeff,'' Kenny finished, spitting out the name.

Binky turned to the source of the voice. ''Actually,''
the man said with a smirk, ''I'm here to interview Jeff
for the *Times*. But if you're nice to me, I'll mention that
a small group of protestors attended the rollout of
Breeze's new scent, but they were outnumbered . . . what
would you say?''—he took the tester from Binky's
hands and fingered it idly—''about a million to one?''
Binky snatched the bottle back before the man could

spray his wrists. Smirk still in place, the man sailed off blithely.

"Screw you, Blatt!" Kenny shouted after the retreating form.

"Explain, please," Binky demanded of Doan.

"Oh, that. That's Barry Blatt. He's the official homosexual at the *San Francisco Times*. Gay story? Send Barry. I'm surprised they sent him to interview a closet case like Jeff Breeze."

"So we may read in tomorrow's paper that Breeze is gay?"

Doan patted her on the head. "Such an innocent! Of course not. Our friend Mr. Blatt has realized that the real riches of the writing world lie in doing up flattering profiles for magazines like *Pendennis,* magazines which never, ever reveal sordid truths about their cover subjects. Oops!" Doan said, looking at Kenny. "I forgot I'm not supposed to get you started on *Pendennis*."

"That magazine has put four—four!—closeted fags on the cover this year. And was there any reference in any of these deep, searching profiles to their real sex lives? No!"

"Calm down, dear," Doan advised. "You may write for *Pendennis* someday."

Kenny snorted. "Not likely."

"Uh," Binky groaned, suddenly weak.

"What? Where?" Doan demanded, aware that their taste in men was the same and also aware that his friend only made that noise for top-of-the-line beef.

Binky pointed, and Doan summarily groaned as well. The man was tall. The man was big. He was putting a cell phone into one pocket of his baggy fatigues while fitting on a headset walkie-talkie. The baggy fatigues would have been an immediate turnoff had it not been for what was above them: six feet, three inches of chiseled beef in a white, too-tight T-shirt, massive pecs and tan biceps popping out all over. Best of all, this dark-

eyed, olive-skinned eighth wonder had a face to die for.
Cheekbones to put Jeff Breeze's to shame, plump,
carved lips over a Kirk Douglas chin, eyebrows thick at
the nose and tapering off like bird wings.

"Must . . . have . . . now," Binky managed to grunt.

"So you can break his heart like you broke Luke's,
leaving him useless even to those of us willing to clean
up your seconds? No way, dearie, this one's mine."

"Forget it," Kenny sliced the air. "That's Sam Braverman, professional thug."

"Thug? How do you know from thugs?" Doan asked.
Since acquiring his detective's license, Doan had become eager to meet more disreputable people in order
to feel more authentic, and this looked like someone
he'd be eager to meet under any circumstances.

"He's Jeff Breeze's chief of security. He's worked
for every sleaze in Hollywood. He keeps their names *out*
of the papers, if you know what I mean."

"Ah, a *fixer*," Doan said, hoping he'd gotten the
lingo right.

Binky didn't care who this man worked for, or what
he did. She was making a beeline for him before her
chance was gone.

"Hey," she said casually to the hunk of her dreams.

He turned around and smiled at her, slaying her instantly. Up close she got the full effect of the soaring
cheekbones, finely drawn eyebrows, long black eye-
lashes, a full-figured but still graceful nose, and eyes of
Mediterranean green, all the more striking against his
softly burnished olive skin.

"Hey yourself."

"Listen," she said, "I'm working this show, but I get
off as soon as this Breeze guy is outta here. Can I buy
you a drink?"

Sam Braverman smiled. "Lady, if I let every
woman—or man—who wanted to get a little closer to
Jeff Breeze buy me a drink, I'd be an alcoholic."

He watched her carefully, smiling a perfectly carved little smile at the dawning look of horror on her face. She hadn't seemed like the type to use him to get to Breeze, but you never knew.

"Oh my god!" she gasped. "No! Are you kidding? I have absolutely no interest in Jeff Breeze. None! Ask my friends over there!" she nearly begged him, pointing at Doan and Kenny. Doan waved; Kenny flipped them the bird and waved his sign. "They *hate* Jeff Breeze, see, so I'm sort of constitutionally obligated to hate him too. But I saw *you*, and . . . well . . ."

Sam laughed. "You're telling the truth. And I'd love to have a drink with you, but I work for Jeff, and he's flying back to L.A. right after this appearance. Since I'm his chief of security, that means I have to go back, too." Noticing the crestfallen look on her face, he pulled out his wallet and handed her his card. "However, if you're ever in L.A. and feeling lonely . . ."

Binky snatched it. "What are you doing this weekend?" she quipped as she read on the card:

SAMOTHRACE BRAVERMAN
Personal Security

"Samothrace?" she asked.

"My father was Greek," he explained. "My mother was Israeli."

Binky swooned. "Oh my god, you *are* perfect."

He laughed. "You need to work on your come-on, you know that? You're making it easy for me to take advantage of you."

"Yes, that is exactly what I am doing."

Sam was distracted from these easy pickings by a squawk from his headset. "Nice to meet you, but I've got to go to work. Call me, okay?"

"Count on it," she said, but he was already moving. She returned to her two scowling compatriots, their

disapproval plain—Doan's for her having thrown over
Luke only to fall for his identical twin; Kenny's for her
having had anything to do with Jeff Breeze, Inc. "We
have a date next time I'm in L.A."

"I take it you're packing your bag?" Doan asked.

"Can I borrow your charge card?" she asked.

"Oh, no! If you're going to do this to Luke, you're
going to do it without any help from me."

"Omigod here he comes!" a girl shrieked as a black
limousine wheeled around the corner, Sam one of several men running alongside it like Secret Service to keep
the crowds away. Binky got her first look at Jeff Breeze,
standing up through the sunroof, waving at the crowd.
She found it hard to figure out if Breeze really had star
power, or if he was merely functioning as a lightning
rod for the unfulfilled sexual fantasies of so many people. He was certainly nothing much to look at in her
book after Sam Braverman; she noted cynically that he
stared straight ahead as he waved, making sure everybody got to see his famous profile. She checked it
against the tester she had somehow managed to hang
onto all this time: yep, it was him.

"Sorry, I've got to borrow this," Kenny said, snatch-
ing the tester out of her hands.

"Hey!" she shouted indignantly, to no avail. Kenny
was gone after Breeze with the tester.

Doan grabbed her arm and hustled her along after
him. "Come on, this is going to be good!"

How Kenny got through the phalanx of gay men, the
legion of teenage girls, and the battalion of security people would be a mystery many would be trying to solve
over the next several days (actually, he'd attached himself to the camera guy from *Hard Copy,* who was used
to performing such infiltrations on a daily basis). But
once through them, and face to face with one of America's sweethearts, Kenny did not hesitate. "Closet case!
Closet case!" he shouted into the cameras. "This man

is *gay! Gay, gay gay!* They oughta call this stuff 'Closet'!" And with that he turned on a startled—and much shorter in person—Jeff Breeze and spritzed him in the face with a huge dose of that fresh, woodsy scent with just a hint of citrus. Breeze responded by blinking, putting a hand to his throat, moving his lips like a fish, and collapsing.

If pandemonium had reigned before this, pure chaos took over. Before the first scream of terror from the crowd had ended, Sam Braverman had hoisted Breeze over one shoulder, thrown him back into the limousine, and shouted "Go! go!" to the driver. Another security person had thrown a stunned Kenny to the ground, and took advantage of the chaos, as security types so often do, to beat him up. Cameras were adding to the body count, clubbing bystanders in the head (nearly missing the quick-reflexed Binky) as they swung around wildly to capture the ratings-boosting carnage.

"Come on," Doan whispered. "There will shortly be too much authority around here for anybody's good. Security!" he shouted, "coming through!" This having achieved nothing, he unabashedly resorted to elbowing his way against the tide of the crowd, which was surging toward the scene of the crime, most of its members unaware that something horrible had just happened.

Somehow, he managed to get her out and away. "God, how ghastly!" he said. "Breeze must have had an allergic reaction to his own perfume. Let's take a minute to savor the rich irony of that, shall we?"

Binky decided she'd rather take a moment to have a cigarette. "Shit! My purse is still inside Macy's. We'll have to go back."

"We'll go back tomorrow. Unless you want to hang around there for a couple of hours, waiting for the cops to get around to you just so they can ask you how Kenny got the tester."

"No, that I do not want to do. I'll just call the charge

card companies and cancel my cards; that way I won't have to go back at all.''

"Now, won't *that* be suspicious?'' Doan asked. "You know, your policeman friend is going to remember that we were with Kenny. Sooner or later you *are* going to have to talk to the cops; I'm just trying to spare you six hours of sitting around today.''

Binky remembered Luke's friend Chuck. "Shit. Shit shit shit! I should have known this would happen! I should *never, ever* have taken a job!''

Doan rolled his eyes. "Come on, let's get you a drink.''

While the working world looked no better through a martini glass, at least the alcohol removed the sharper edges from her day's experience. The Detour was, as it is at all hours, reliably dark and thus easy on frazzled nerves.

"Two more, please, Steve,'' Doan asked his favorite bartender.

"Comin' up. Did you guys hear about Jeff Breeze?''

"Yeah, we were there.''

"Wow. Of all people, I never thought Kenny Wells would end up a murderer.''

"Murderer!'' Doan and Binky both gasped.

"Yeah, I thought you were there.''

"He collapsed, that was all.'' Doan turned to Binky for confirmation. "Wasn't it?''

"I just heard it on the radio before I got here,'' Steve said. "Jeff Breeze is dead.''

Doan and Binky looked at each other silently for a moment before Doan said what was on both their minds: "Here we go again.''

THREE

The last time that the force of nature that was Doan descended on the Hall of Justice, it had been to rescue a paramour from the clutches of a justice system gone awry. The blood and thunder that Doan had been capable of supplying in the name of love was absent today, replaced by a brisk professionalism—even though, strictly speaking, this wasn't a professional visit; as Binky had reminded him, Kenny was not the sort of wealthy client Doan had dangled before her eyes when he'd talked her into becoming a detective.

"I know, darling, but just imagine *la publicité* if we catch Jeff Breeze's real killer!"

"Sure, with about as much benefit as we got out of catching the SoMa Killer."

"That was different," Doan said. "For all the danger to life and limb that we went through, to the rest of the world it was still just a quaint, charming story about the goings-on in a quaint, charming town. Now we're talkin' movie stars!" he finished, so exultantly that Binky decided not to remind him that the danger to life and limb had not been as great as all that.

"Nevertheless, don't you think it's a bit early in our career to be taking on pro bono work?"

"Here we are!" he announced brightly as their cab pulled up at the jail, dodging any further verbal bullets.

Inside, Doan was dismayed to learn that his interview with Kenny would have to be conducted over a phone, facing Kenny through security glass. "If that is the case," he demanded huffily, "why can't I just call down here and talk to him on the phone?"

"Prisoners aren't allowed phone privileges," the bored desk sergeant said.

Doan shuddered at the thought of life without a phone—that, he felt sure, was cruel and unusual punishment. "Unless I'm here in person," he asked sarcastically, "in which case he and I get to make the world's shortest-distance call?"

Normally, he would have simply picked up the phone (a real one) and called Luke, who could have easily arranged a private interview room for a face-to-face conversation with Kenny—and what good is power, Doan believed, if you don't use it to help your friends? But Binky had insisted that Luke had done them all the favors he was going to do, and so Doan subjected himself to the rare and humiliating experience of having to follow the rules. Binky, meanwhile, was taking this opportunity to give her statement to the cops as to what she'd seen the previous day.

Kenny was ushered into the room and sat down across the glass from Doan. He picked up the phone. "Collect call from Hell, will you accept the charges?"

"Glad to see you haven't lost your sense of humor. You know, it's true—everybody *does* look better under arrest!"

"Yeah, but the kind of dates I could get in here aren't exactly what I'm looking for. Doan, I really appreciate your coming down here. I mean, we don't really know each other that well, but it's nice to have a visitor. . . ."

Doan sobered up. It was strange to see how different Kenny was now from the Kenny who'd been so obnoxious at Macy's the previous day. But Doan had seen many kind, well-intentioned people turn into angry shouting beasts when they found a cause. An irritating indignation, more irritating for having been emphasized for effect, seemed to walk hand in hand with protesting. Doan usually kept these thoughts to himself, though, especially in a town where protesting was one of the most popular recreational activities. "Kinda scary in there, huh?"

"A little. It's actually more like joining a bad fraternity. Which is not to say I'd want to graduate to a penitentiary or anything."

"And you won't, darling, I promise you."

"Promises, promises."

"Listen, the last time I was in the hoosegow—I mean, *at* the hoosegow—oh, you know what I mean. Last time I said to somebody, 'I'll get you out of here,' damn all if I didn't do just that. You see, Binky and I are taking your case."

"You've always been full of surprises, Doan, but I never knew you were a lawyer."

"No, no!" Doan said, horrified at the thought. "We're detectives. We're going to find out who really killed Jeff Breeze."

"Looks like it was me, doesn't it?"

"Well, yes, it does. But while we may not know each other that well, I know you're not a killer." Doan pulled out pen and paper. "Now, I hate to ask you the same things the cops already asked, but I'm supposed to do this as if I couldn't just lift the phone and get the inside scoop. So what did you tell them?"

"That I didn't kill him. That went over well."

"What did they ask you?"

"Where I got the bottle. What poison I put into it."

"Did you tell them you got it from Binky? The bottle,

I mean. That she got it at random from some crate full of them inside Macy's?''

"Sure. And I told them everybody who'd handled it. They'll be calling you, I'm afraid." Doan waved Kenny's concerns away idly. He'd promised Binky no help from Luke . . . on the case, that is; surely she couldn't begrudge Doan's turning to Luke for help when Doan himself was about to be questioned as a material witness to a murder. "So I told them everybody who handled it. Me, you, Binky.''

"And we can all testify that you didn't touch it until you yanked it out of Binky's hands and sprayed Breeze only a minute later. So why do they still have you in here?''

"According to them, I had plenty of time while fighting my way through the crowd to unscrew the top and put in whatever killed him. Have you heard anything about what it was?''

"No. Do you have a lawyer yet?''

"So I'm told. Some minimum-wage public defender who could give a rat's ass. I haven't seen him yet.''

Promises were promises, Doan thought, but this was intolerable. How was he to operate a successful business without using his vast web of connections, a web whose threads just happened at this current moment all to lead to Luke Faraglione? It was unthinkable that he should go behind Binky's back, but they would get nowhere without a little official help, and Doan was determined to get it.

"The toxicology screen probably hasn't come back yet anyway," Doan said. "Once it does, I'll call you. . . . I mean, dammit, I'll drag my ass down here again and let you know." Doan had a flash. "No, the hell I will! I'm getting you a lawyer. A *good* one. And he'll tell you. *He'll* be allowed to see you in person.''

"I'm amazed you even got to see me at all. The guards tell me the media's clamoring to interview me, and you know me, I'm ready to talk to them all! So how'd you get in?''

"Well, let's jes' say we is kinfolk for a spell, and leave it at that." He put away his unused pen and paper.

"And I never thought I'd see the day you used the phrase 'toxicology screen'!"

Doan laughed. "Isn't it amazing what important facts you can find crammed into your head when you actually need them?" he said, neglecting to mention that all he knew about toxicology screens came from watching *Law and Order*. He got up. "Now, you hang tight, honey. I'm not saying we'll have you out of here in a jiffy, but believe me, we'll get you out."

It wouldn't be fair to Doan to say that he didn't feel guilty about breaking his promise to Binky. Nonetheless, it *would* be fair to say that he had cleverly rationalized his way into calling Luke for information essential to the case. Which, after all, was more important: to placate a stubborn person who refused to have anything to do with the one man in the universe who was perfect for her, or to save a man unjustly accused of murder? Doan knew his friendship with Binky would survive were she to find out about his deception (although their new business relationship would undoubtedly collapse), but was there anybody else who could help Kenny?

It was with this in mind that he'd arranged to meet Luke the next day. Now let it be said that Luke Faraglione was not the kind of cop to leak information at random; however, he knew Doan, and he knew that if Doan said somebody was innocent, well, that person just might be innocent. Let it also be confessed that Luke felt obligated to Doan for helping him in his unsuccessful siege of Binky's ramparts. So Luke didn't hesitate to give Doan the information—after all, he knew damn well that in the case of a murdered movie star, even if he didn't spill the beans, some tabloid would pay somebody at the coroner's office a fortune for the autopsy results. And so it was that he pushed a clasp envelope across the table to Doan, who greedily opened it and began scanning the report.

"Blah blah blah. I don't get it. What did he die of?"

"Asphyxiation, brought on by some element they haven't identified yet."

Doan whistled. "So he really was poisoned, hmm?"

"Definitely. It doesn't look good for your friend."

Doan sighed, feeling momentarily defeated. But that didn't last. "No, no, no. He couldn't have done it. Not intentionally. You've seen Kenny, haven't you?" Luke nodded. "He's in shock—a dead Jeff Breeze is the very last thing in the world he expected." His faith in his friend restored, he pressed on. "Anything else in that autopsy?"

Luke laughed. "I think you'll get a kick out of this." He pointed to a list. "Things found in Jeff Breeze besides poison."

Doan's eyes widened as he went down the list, then narrowed. "Hmph. Cheekbone implants. Jaw implants. Wisdom teeth pulled—that could be to enhance the cheekbones," he enlightened Luke. "Pectoral implants! This is too much."

"It gets better," Luke assured him.

"Oh my god—a penile implant? Wow, when you go in for an autopsy in this town, they really take you apart."

"Actually, the guy who did it found the pec implants first, then decided to see what else he could find."

"Liposuction scars. Eye tuck scars. Plugs? Jeff Breeze had *hair plugs?* Was there anything *not* artificial about this guy?"

"The tox screen also found human growth hormone."

"Steroids, eh? I shouldn't wonder."

"Not exactly. It's supposed to be for people with

AIDS who're suffering from wasting syndrome—helps them add muscle.''

''Yeah, ole Jeffie was really wasting away, wasn't he?'' A light bulb went on in Doan's head. ''Hey, did they test him for HIV?''

''No. No point if he's dead.''

''Well, there certainly is a point,'' Doan said angrily. ''If he was positive, then Kenny was right—this guy was leading a double life. And you, Detective Faraglione, should know that a man leading a double life can have enemies nobody in his other life knows about.''

''That's true; unfortunately, the coroner didn't have consent to do the HIV test, and the body's been shipped back to L.A. for the funeral. Here's a tip for you—if this guy had secret enemies, they might show up at the funeral. Killers do that sometimes, you know—they need closure as much as the grieving relatives do.''

''So you're saying we should hightail it down to L.A. for the funeral?''

''Jeff Breeze was killed up here, but if somebody besides Kenny Wells had a reason for wanting him dead, chances are that person is where Breeze lived and worked—L.A. If you want clues, that's where you're going to have to look.''

Back at home, lying on the couch, Doan sighed heavily. Catching the SoMa Killer had been taxing, but it hadn't meant leaving San Francisco for a city quite so completely its opposite. S.F. was easygoing, laid-back to the point of comatose; L.A. was hard-driving and competitive. S.F. was a bit schlubby, a place where a few extra pounds didn't mean the difference between a happy life and social exile; L.A. demanded perpetual worship at the temple of the bitchin' bod. S.F. had plenty of room for eccentrics like Doan, who may raise eyebrows but who were also inarguably good for tourism; L.A. viewed eccentrics as, basically, bad box office—someone like

Doan might play in an art house, but he could never open a film in Peoria.

Most of all, S.F. was possessed of a shabby public transit system that basically disappeared nights and weekends, whereas L.A. was possessed of almost no public transportation at all ... and neither Binky nor Doan knew how to drive. In a child-size city like San Francisco, it was possible for our frivolous spenders to get around in cabs without making too great an impact on the budget, but the distances in the Southland, as well as their dearth of cabs, were problematic. Doan hadn't anticipated having to make this trip; if he had, would he have promised Kenny his freedom so eagerly?

He picked up the phone and dialed. "Hello?" Binky answered.

"Do you still want to see your new friend Mr. Braverman this weekend?"

"Hell, yes."

"Then pack your bag. We've got a funeral to attend."

FOUR

Stepping off the plane, Doan realized he might have dreaded L.A. unnecessarily. After all, certain facts became blazingly apparent immediately. For one, the weather was nicer, even if the air was worse. Nothing cheered Doan up like a warm summer's day, and L.A. often had those even in the dead of winter. He was starting to think things might not be so bad, when Binky took a wrong turn away from the Super Shuttle station and toward the plethora of rent-a-car agencies.

"What do you think you're doing?" he asked her.

"Something very Doan-like, actually. I'm surprised you didn't think of it yourself."

Doan paled. "You're going to rent a car."

"Yep."

"But you don't have a driver's license!"

"I have a California ID, which looks exactly like a license, and which most fools behind counters don't examine too closely."

"All right. All right. Say you *do* rent a car. Since you don't know how to drive, what do you plan to do with it?"

"I've ridden in plenty of cars," she said confidently. "Besides, I almost learned to drive when I was sixteen. Everything but parallel parking. I'm sure it'll all come back to me."

"Are you, now. I feel so reassured. Okay, Miss Smarty, here's a test for you. You're on the freeway. You suddenly realize you've got to make a turnoff that's racing up on you, and you're three lanes over. You bolt over, nearly causing an accident. You get on the turnoff and suddenly somebody is following you—somebody you cut off. What do you do?"

"I shoot him, right? I mean, when in Rome . . ."

Doan gave up. "Fine. Go ahead. There are six car agencies here. I'll just sit here and fume while you make a fool of yourself in all six, trying to rent a car without a driver's license."

He didn't have to wait long. Binky returned from the first agency to dangle a set of keys before his eyes. "God help us," he whispered.

"Don't sweat it. Look, Doan, you know there's no way we can get around this town without a car. Well, now we've got one. I don't see why you of all people are so upset about somebody bending the rules. After all," she said casually, "isn't that how you got Jeff Breeze's autopsy report?"

"Er, um, well . . ."

"Never mind. I knew you'd probably run to Luke when the going got tough; I just wanted to make sure you didn't run to Luke before the going got tough."

Doan heaved a sigh of relief. "I'm so glad you know. It's such a burden keeping secrets, especially from you."

Binky had rented an unremarkable sedan. She had found it prudent to take the first car offered, rather than allowing the sun to rise over the dim clerk's horizon and illuminate Binky's charade. As he always did, Doan quickly occupied himself pushing the myriad buttons that controlled the seat, the windows, the air conditioner, the stereo. . . .

"Please stop fidgeting with the dashboard," Binky requested.

"Sorry." He occupied himself looking out the window as Binky tried to figure out how to drive. "*R*, that must be for reverse," she decided aloud, to which Doan only added a small whimper. Sure enough, reverse it was, and Binky brought a surprisingly light touch to the gas pedal. Soon, to Doan's amazement, they were on the road with only occasional jerks and starts to dismay him.

"Well now, if you know how to drive, why didn't you ever get a license?" he asked her.

"Believe it or not, I made an astonishingly mature decision. See, when I was sixteen and learning how to drive, I would get so angry on the road that if someone cut me off, well, I *would* have shot them if I'd had a gun. I realized I didn't have the temperament to deal rationally with maniacs, so I decided not to drive. What's your excuse?"

"Mother and father tried to teach me how to drive, but you know how well I follow the commands of others. Every time we got into the car, we just fought and fought. It wasn't worth it. Then I moved to San Francisco, where it's nice to have a car, but you don't really need one, and I never knew anybody who had one, so I just, sort of, unintentionally never learned to drive."

"Well, I'll give you lessons, if you like."

Doan bit back the font of sarcasm trying to gush from his lips. "Once you get your own license, I'm sure you'll be a wonderful teacher."

Binky shrugged. "Your loss. By the way, where are we staying?"

Doan pulled a map out of his backpack and unfolded it. "Umm, turn left on La Cienega."

"Where are we going, Doan?" she pressed.

"You'll see."

Binky groaned. Having known people who'd actually done things with their lives, such as starting new businesses, she knew that things had to be done on the cheap at the outset. Never having stayed in cheap lodgings in her entire life, she was not quite sure she was prepared for the experience. They were in L.A., after all, and visions of the less appealing sets from her favorite film noir classics came unbidden to mind. What little stick-to-itiveness she possessed was rapidly being eroded by visions of lumpy mattresses, cockroaches, neon signs buzzing outside the window, and, most frightening of all, no room service. Surely no future reward for enduring such suffering could make up for the horror of having to get dressed and leave one's room *before* coffee.

But Doan's directions seemed to be leading them not toward flatness, grayness, and squalor, but through ever-increasing wealth and ever more magnificent palm trees. Driving past a park, she recognized a good half-dozen Botero statues, the sort of expensive artworks reserved for well-guarded museums. It was certainly a telling indicator of the community's wealth that they could afford to populate a park (for there were no people currently in the park, and probably never were) with such conspicuous consumables. "Is this Beverly Hills?" she asked Doan.

"The very same. Turn right here."

Now Binky had never been to Los Angeles before, but a certain radar she had inherited from her patrician family told her that this large pink building they were approaching was the repository of luxury and ease. As her ancestors had done ever since there had been cars, she pulled up to the front of the hotel, confidently expecting that someone young and extremely good-looking would open her door for her and park her car, and that is just what happened. The bags she had struggled with at the airports were whisked ahead of her by yet another future soap star; the door was opened for her and Doan by magic hands; and a gust of perfectly conditioned air welcomed her inside. She found her brain starting to relax as it filled with the pleasant buzz that comes in places made of money.

"We can't possibly afford this," she rebuked Doan mildly, too relieved at her narrow escape from the No-Tell Motel to worry too much about consequences at this point.

"Ah, but McCandler Van de Kamp Inc., can." He proudly whipped out two gold Visas with that name on both, each also with their own names.

"How did you get a gold Visa?" she asked accusingly.

"Well, you know how banks are. They don't really care if you can *afford* another Visa, the only important question is, have you made your payments on time on the Visas you already have? And I have, so here it is."

She stopped in the middle of the lobby, arms folded. "I will now stand here and wait for the actual explanation."

He laughed. "Eleanor cosigned for me!"

"Aha!" she cried. All was now clear; Eleanor Van Owens was the immensely rich woman and long-time friend of Doan's whom they rescued in our last episode, after her husband and his accomplice had kidnapped her. "And when the bill comes due?"

He shrugged. "By that time, we'll have solved the murder. And *this* time, we're going to make some money off it. I set Kenny up with Martin Hart for his lawyer," he said, naming his friend the powerhouse attorney, another friend of Doan's, "and Martin is also handling book and film rights to the whole story. This time, dear, we are assured of our just reward."

This mollified Binky, especially as it appeared that their just reward was to begin now, in a bungalow at the Beverly Hills Hotel, rather than later, after much sacrifice, suffering, and just plain inconvenience.

Binky picked up the phone and uttered the three most beautiful words in the English language. "Hello, room service?"

Doan took the phone away from her and hung it up. "Later, dear. Right now we've got to go pay our respects to the dear departed dead."

"What's the holdup?" Doan asked, distracted from his button-fiddling (this time with the stereo).

"I don't know. Some kind of roadblock."

"Then we must be here." He reached into his bag, pulled out something bright orange, and jumped out of the car.

"Hey!" Binky called. Doan ignored her, putting the orange thing—which turned out to be a sign with FU-NERAL written on it in large black letters—under the windshield wipers.

"There!" he said after getting back in. "Now we're part of the procession. Go on around these cars now; we'll get through."

"Ingenious," Binky muttered, crossing the double line and passing the honking motorists. "We're with the funeral," she said blandly to the cop at the barricade.

"Sorry," he said, "nobody's getting through right now. Too many people."

"Omigod, look at that!" Doan said, his face a mask of awe right out of a Spielberg movie. Laid out on a bier like an Eastern potentate of yore was Jeff Breeze, his handsome profile on display one last time. And behind this cortege were countless weeping fans, later estimated in the hundreds of thousands by the local news.

"God," Doan muttered, "I don't think this town has seen anything like this since Valentino. Listen, we're going to have to park and walk, like the rest of this rabble."

"Where do you expect me to park?" she asked testily.

"This is Los Angeles, darling; where we have convenience stores, they have parking garages. Look, there's one there!"

"It's full," Binky said, her eagle eye reading the sign blocking the entrance.

"Damn. Well, just double-park, that's what all these people must have done."

"All right, but if we come back and the car's been towed?"

"I'll assume complete responsibility, okay? We'll just have to hope our Funeral sign gets them to leave it alone. Let's go!"

Nobody prevented them from joining the horde of mourners walking behind Breeze's cortege. People were throwing flowers on the bier, which only fell off, overloaded with flowers as it already was. Walking beside the bier was a woman in black, her long blond hair tucked up under a black hat straight off Alexis Carrington. Doan indicated her to Binky. "The widow, Jennifer Breeze."

"Where are we going?" Binky asked as the stately procession headed down Hollywood Boulevard.

"He and the missus were members of that loony cult. Remember Evgenia Dollars?"

Binky did indeed remember the name. Back at boarding school, Evgenia Dollars had been the favorite author of a certain type of girl: smart, but prone to romantic fantasies about heroic men; loners, drawn to Dollars's portraits of beautiful social exiles, characters whose greed, enshrined by Dollars as their virtue, was probably the real reason they were so damn lonely. Proud, lonely women who stood above the mere carrion of humanity, and who were only happy being raped by proud, lonely men. Her books invariably ended with one of her long diatribes against fellow feeling and sympathy, crammed into the mouth of one of her characters. Born Evgenia Andropov in Russia, Dollars had fled Communism and her proper name for America, where her rationalization of unfettered capitalism as the greatest good for the smallest number, as well as her startling facility with the English language, had made her a best-selling author in the forties and fifties.

A lifelong atheist, near the end of her life she had organized the Church of Dollars, ostensibly devoted to the unquestioning worship of one's self, but really just a tax dodge that allowed her to disseminate her "philosophy" without paying taxes on the royalties. Since her death, the Church of Dollars itself had morphed into a self-realization cult, borrowing from est, Scientology, and every other "me" movement of the last thirty years.

At the beginning of the eighties, the church had moved from New York to Los Angeles, partly because the unfettered greed espoused by Dollars had been made flesh by a Republican president, whose influence quickly made New York a city teeming with the homeless mentally ill and deranged crack addicts. But mostly, the church had moved because of one man: Ted Trask, a seventies' sitcom superstar who'd made the rare transition from TV to movies, and who ascribed his success entirely to himself and his faithful following of Evgenia Dollars's teachings.

Evgenia may have been a visionary, but even she never prophesied the value of celebrity in the promotion of one's ideas. However, those church elders in whose hands she had left her empire upon her ascent to her heavenly platinum throne were not slow to realize that interest in the church had risen dramatically after Trask's public espousal of it, and one of them had the bright idea of moving the whole operation to Hollywood, where self-interest was the universal watchword.

"We're headed toward the Church of Dollars, aren't we?" Binky groaned.

"The very same." Doan sighed. Now, the milk of human kindness was a relatively dry spring in both

Binky and Doan, who had done reasonably well for themselves and expected others to do the same. But the doctrine of the Church of Dollars was, well, just plain mean. Hungry? Get a job! Homeless? Get a job! Jobless? Get a job! Dollars's philosophy was admirably suited for people for whom nothing had ever gone wrong, and who believed that no great misfortune could ever befall them which would require the assistance of another, more compassionate, human being.

The cortege finally drew to a halt before a gleamingly restored art deco building. Dollars had fetishized deco as the embodiment of her characters—streamlined, sleek, in perpetual motion. The Temple of Our Lady of Immediate Gratification loomed large and pink over Hollywood Boulevard, a street better known for the industrious capitalism of its illegal economy than for spiritual appropriateness. In fact, many were the tourists who'd mistaken it for the Frederick's of Hollywood museum. Were it not for the genuine platinum-coated dollar sign that turned atop the "spire," the temple might well have been mistaken for a grand old movie palace, and with good reason: Dollars had written more than once about the impact American movies had made on her young Russian soul, and she'd even toiled in the vineyards of Hollywood for a while, cranking out scripts that, to her perpetual rage, were never brought to the screen exactly as she'd written them.

"Now how are we going to get past these people," Binky asked, "let alone actually get in?" The swollen crowd had met its match in L.A.'s finest, who manned the barricades, assisting the minions of the church as they checked names off the guest list. It was a large list, but even so, the funeral had become the town's hottest ticket. Simply *everybody* was going in.

"It's like the Academy Awards!" Doan enthused, rather than answering Binky's question. "All they need is tuxes and a red carpet. Look, there's even paparazzi!"

Sure enough, many of the somberly dressed stars were stopping with their dates to pose for the photographers. "Come on," he said, pulling her into the maelstrom. "You're going to find out why I had you dress for the occasion. Coming through!" he shouted.

Sure enough, just as the Irish once fell to their knees at the sight of a black cassock, so the mob parted for a pair of glamorous women clad in Armani from their sunglasses to their socks. At the police line, Doan waved to one of the clipboard wielders. "Would you please tell Sam Braverman that Binky Van de Kamp is here to see him?"

"I—" Binky began to protest, but a hard squeeze from Doan silenced her.

"He's rather busy right now," the man said, not at all impressed with the pair's fashion élan. "Is he expecting you?"

"Yes," Doan said confidently. "Please hurry."

The gatekeeper pulled a cellular phone the size of a candy bar from his jacket and muttered into it. Then he eyed them again before saying into the phone, "Two women, one with a blond bob, one with long, light brown hair. Both well dressed." He listened. "Right." He hung up, smiled for the first time. "He'll be out in a minute."

Binky and Doan had only seen the tower of beef that was Sam Braverman in his activewear; Sam Braverman dressed for a funeral was something else entirely. He was, daringly, *not* in Armani but in what Doan suspected to be Brooks Brothers. The dark, blocky suit enhanced his already massive shoulders and gave him an air of supreme authority. Without the mirrored sunglasses he'd worn at their last encounter, the brilliant blaze of his eyes was apparent from the time he emerged from the temple.

"So you decided to take me up on my offer," he said, smiling at Binky.

"How could I keep away?"

"I must have had a powerful effect on you, to bring you down here, and get you to fight through all these people just to see me."

Binky took off her sunglasses to deliver to Sam the full force of her lust. "Ain't no mountain high enough," she said, gazing up raptly.

At this point, Doan thought it advisable to cut in. "We hope you can help us," he said briskly. "I suppose you know the name Kenny Wells?"

"I certainly do. He killed Jeff Breeze."

"We don't think so." As rehearsed, he and Binky showed their licenses as if they were Scully and Mulder. "Mr. Wells has retained us to find the real killer."

Much to Doan's surprise, Sam took the wallet out of his hand and examined the license. He looked at Doan and smiled; Doan flushed—Sam had obviously not been sure Doan was a man until he'd seen the *M* on the license. Now, most people on this earth would have laughed a drag queen and his fag hag right out of there simply out of amusement at their presumption at being crime solvers. Fortunately for our heroes, Sam had spent enough time in Hollywood not to take anything, or anyone, at face value.

"And you thought Jeff Breeze's funeral would be a good place to look for suspects."

"That's correct," Doan said, refusing to blush again. "We'd certainly appreciate your help with this. I'm sure you're as eager as we are to put your former employer's killer away."

Sam smiled lazily. "You might not know it from all this," he said, indicating the crowd, "but this is a funeral. It really wouldn't be appropriate for people to be asking questions of the guests."

"Well," Binky offered, "what if we keep our mouths shut and just observe?"

Sam pondered this for a moment. "How do I know you'll keep that promise?"

Binky upped the wattage of her lust for Sam's benefit. "Because the last thing I'd want would be for you to be mad at me."

Sam laughed. "Okay. Come on."

Amazed at the good fortune that had accompanied their act of bravado, they followed Sam down the sidewalk to the temple. "You know," Binky whispered to Doan, "we just might have what it takes to be detectives after all."

FIVE

The interior of the Temple of Our Lady of Immediate Gratification was a cross between an art deco train station and Salt Lake City's Mormon Tabernacle. The walls were adorned with pastel murals that stood Socialist Realism on its head—below, beautiful blond workers of both sexes, next, the Capitalist, the Great Man of Evgenia Dollars's philosophy, and above all these upturned faces, the almighty dollar, glowing like God in a Renaissance painting, surrounded by heavenly courtiers in the form of yen, deutsche mark, pounds, and other stable and prestigious world currencies.

"Did you model for that mural?" Doan asked Binky, who replied by kicking him in the heel. "Ow! That's not fair. You do look like a heroine out of a Dollars novel, you know."

"Yep, that's me, the proverbial fallow field, just waiting to be ploughed by some titan of industry." She looked around the crowd. "I don't know who any of these people are."

"Then you obviously don't read enough movie magazines. There's Charlotte Kane," he said, pointing at a willowy brunette. "Former child star, smart as a whip, she directs now as much as she acts. Big ole D, according to Kenny."

"Really?"

"Yup. And, she's got a black lover she keeps squirreled away in an apartment in Paris. America may be ready for homosexuality, but interracial homosexuality? Not yet, and she knows it. Supercloseted."

"Who's she talking to?"

"What a pretty picture! That's Ted Trask."

Binky well knew who Trask was. A TV star as a teenager, he'd gone on to star in the last dying gasp of the Hollywood musical in the seventies, then his career had sunk like a stone in the eighties, seemingly never to rise again as the tabs spread rumors about his affair with the male nanny of his (adopted) children. Now he'd staged a comeback; older, wiser, and much fatter, he'd wisely become a "character actor" and was working in Hollywood again.

A large, imposing woman in a black suit put her hands out to Trask and Kane, embracing them in this moment of sorrow. "Who's that with them?" Binky asked.

"Here, let me check my crib sheet," Doan said, pulling a folded paper out of a perfectly stitched pocket. "Kenny helped me make it. I held up copies of magazines to the glass and he told me which pictures to cut out. Prison requires such inventiveness! I think it brings out the best in him." Sure enough, the paper held some glossy mag shots of various unidentifiables, along with a brief note. "There. That's Mary Duveen. Major, major publicist."

"Did she work for Breeze?"

"And everybody else who's commanding more than one million dollars a picture. Piss her off and you're toast in this town. Now surely you know that accomplished actress over there!"

Doan indicated the widow Breeze, dressed in black

with a black veil. "Very tasteful," Doan murmured.
"Very Jackie O." She stood by the open casket, running
a receiving line for accepting condolences. Binky had
her second look at Jeff Breeze in person—whatever
grisly death rictus he may have endured in his final seconds had been wiped away and replaced with a seraphic
smile, presumably at the thought of the foreign grosses
for *Total Carnage*, a formula thriller and Breeze's last
movie, which everybody thought had peaked but which
got new legs after the actor's death.

Mary Duveen said something to Trask and Kane that
made them flinch. Trask set her face with a look of
loathing, but finally both nodded. Duveen literally held
her hand out and snapped her fingers, and sure enough,
someone came running.

"Check the sheet," Binky nudged him.

"Ooohh!"

"Who is it?"

"Nobody, really, not in the big picture. But important
nonetheless. That's Cory Kissell—Kenny calls him
'Cory Kissass.' He writes for your favorite magazine."

"*Pendennis*? Really?"

Doan pointed to the author photo of Kissell clipped
from the front of the magazine. *Pendennis* had started
out as a magazine about the doings of the rich and famous back in the Twenties, but while the Depression
had not taken away people's taste for seeing the rich at
play, our corporate masters had deemed it best that they
should only see made-up rich people in movies, rather
than actual rich people in *Pendennis*, who might have
become the target of focused ire for some several millions of people ruined by the stock market crash. The
magazine of the twenties had, appropriately enough,
been revived in the eighties, and had since then parlayed
into major advertising dollars a successful formula with
which no sane editor ever messed: each issue contained
one celebrity murder case; one "deep" piece on Haiti

or Bosnia which none of the mag's subscribers ever read but which made them feel better about buying it (not unlike being able to say you buy *Playboy* for the articles); one gossipy scandal piece set amongst New York's intelligentsia; and the invariable cover story, a gushing star profile written by Cory Kissass. "And engineered," Doan was saying to Binky, "by Mary Duveen, who only lets her clients be interviewed if they get the cover and if she gets to approve all the questions beforehand. Kenny says that *Pendennis* puts closeted gay stars on its covers all the time. They cover their ass by having Cory only ask people everybody *knows* are queer questions like, 'How would you respond to rumors that you're gay?' and they get to say 'I don't know *how* these rumors get started,' when really the rumors get started because the star was recently spotted in a sling at a fisting orgy."

"Ugh," Binky said. "No details, please."

"And they do *absolutely no fact checking!* I mean, if it's a profile of Mark Carrington"—he named a rich and dumb-as-a-post Republican who served as talking head for his brainier, more ambitious wife—"they'll trot out the big guns: 'Male staffers say Carrington is fond of giving them long hugs,' that kind of insinuating thing. But when it comes to the truth about movie stars, it's hands off."

Both Kane and Trask shook hands with Kissell, who was then quickly shooed away by Duveen. "Huh," Binky said, thinking out loud.

"I'm sorry, that's not a sentence," Doan said. "Please try again."

"You'd think they'd be a little more grateful to someone who helps them stay in the closet."

"Perhaps they despise him for being so very willing to help out."

"If they have a shred of self-respect, I should hope so. Looks like they're seating for the service," she said, indicating an altercation between an usher and a loud, bearded man.

"What the hell do you mean I'm in the fourth pew? Don't you know who I am? I was his best friend in this industry!"

Doan pored over the crib sheet. "That's Mack Maven. He *used to* produce hits one after the other. Now he's a total cokehead and his last three movies have been flops. Breeze dumped him two movies ago. He's lucky to get the fourth pew!"

Rather than arguing, the usher pulled out a cellular phone and dialed. Several feet away, Mary Duveen pulled a cellular phone out and answered it. She promptly headed for the scene of the crisis, nabbing on her way a man in a double-breasted olive suit with a large gold dollar-sign tie clasp. "That's the last of them on this list," Doan said. "That's Ronald Piebald, the rock on which Evgenia built her church. Let's listen in!" Doan said gleefully, tugging Binky toward the impending scene.

But before they got there, a man stumbled into Doan. "Oh!" Doan cried out involuntarily.

"Sorry," the man murmured, steadying himself on Doan's arm. After composing himself, Doan discovered a piece of paper had been put in his hand. He opened it and read it.

"Where did he go?" Doan asked Binky, looking around wildly.

"I don't know. I was watching the scene up there," she replied, indicating Mack Maven. Mary Duveen's back was to them, but Binky saw that something Duveen had said had turned Maven's face ashen, and the argument was over, Maven taking his place in the fourth pew and glad to get it.

"Do you remember what he looked like?"

"I just saw the back of him. Why?"

"Read this," he said, shoving the paper at her:

> If you want to know who killed Jeff Breeze,
> meet me at Club Do It tonight at 11.

The note was unsigned. "Come on," Doan said, "we've got to find that guy." But their efforts were fruitless; the man had gotten lost in the crowd. The hosted bar in the lobby seemed as good a place as any to give up.

"What?!" an indignant woman ahead of them at the bar said to the bartender. She turned away angrily and grabbed a much shorter man. "They're out of Pellegrino! We're leaving."

"Two Bombay Sapphire martinis, please," Doan said, pleased at the economy they were practicing by getting their first martinis of the day free rather than paying ruinous room service prices for them.

While under other circumstances Binky might have noted that it was rather early to start drinking hard liquor, this long day had led her to believe that a stiff one was exactly what she needed. She and Doan clinked glasses and drank up. "Ahhh," they chorused.

"So if we don't know what this guy looks like, how will we find him?" Binky asked.

"I have the feeling he'll find us."

Although the note had called the place Club Do It, the sign outside said, with hype appropriate, if not necessary, in these environs, "Club DO IT!" A quick peek into the alley behind the bar would confirm that, at any given time, several patrons were to be found obeying their hosts' exhortation. Although the bar was a shabby, brick-fronted relic of the Seventies, too old to be shiny but not old enough to be quaint, there was nonetheless a velvet rope behind which stood dozens if not a hundred young men, all so perfectly coiffed that one might think the occupants of the line lived in dread of nothing more than a stiff breeze. Binky found herself practically gasping at the sight of some of these knockouts, omitting the actual sound only because she realized they were, after all, all gay. Having worked in clubs since the age of eighteen, Doan had seen enough astonishing male beauty rise and fall to jade him of it for the most part. Nonetheless, there were some specimens in the line that caused even his jaw to drop. Both suddenly remembered that L.A. was, after all, the farm on which so much beefy beauty was raised to feed the ravenous maw of movies and TV. It was one thing to see a good-looking man on TV, quite another to see so many good-looking men live and in person.

"Every cute guy in the world is here," Binky announced, "and they're all gay."

"If America ever found out that all those wholesome-looking men they see every night are gay, why, they'd rush out here and burn the whole city down!" Doan decided aloud.

"Are we going to have to stand in this line?" Binky asked disconsolately. "They really ought to have a cocktail waitress out here, to serve the people waiting to get in."

"That would probably be illegal," Doan informed her. "And of course we're not waiting in line!" They swept up to the door, where a doorman whose face had suffered a head-on collision with a hardware store held a clipboard. Doan fished something out of his purse, and Binky hastened to pull her detective's license out as well, but then she saw that what he'd produced was a press pass. "Doan McCandler? From the *Watchtower* in San Francisco?"

The man licked his pierced lip with a pierced tongue as he searched the guest list. "Sorry. Not on the list."

"Well, I'm writing a story about nightlife down here, and . . ."

"Then you should have called the manager and gotten on the list. Line's over there."

"Look again," Binky said. "Try Van de Kamp."

The doorman shrugged and flipped through the list again. "Nope."

Finally Doan lost patience and pulled out his detective's license. "Listen. We won't snow you anymore. We're working on the Jeff Breeze murder case and we're supposed to meet an informant here at eleven, which is to say, now. Now, if you'd rather see an innocent kid go to jail than let us in, that's up to you."

He shrugged. "That and a hundred bucks'll get you in."

Unfazed, Doan immediately handed the man a hundred dollar bill. The doorman gave a curt nod to his companion, who pulled the rope aside for Binky and Doan to enter.

"I'll have to remember that," Binky said. "Anytime you go to a club and don't want to wait in line, just fork out a Ben Franklin! I'm surprised more people don't do it."

"Actually," Doan whispered, "having been a doorman myself, I can tell you that most people are too proud to do it—so sure are they that they deserve to be let in on the basis of how fabulous they are. Of course, back home a twenty would do, but I guess there's more money down here. I've found that taking bribes from desperate club patrons is a handy untaxable income source!" he concluded brightly.

The interior of Club DO IT! detoured very little from the formula for a successful gay bar: basically dark, with small spotlights strategically placed to enable those sufficiently sure of their perfection to show off their bone structure for the benefit of the other patrons. Benches lined the walls all around, and mirrors covered the wall behind the bar, so the hunters and the hunted had the best possible view of each other. A small stage would later host avant-garde drag performances; this evening's program was to include a drag tag team manifesting successively the many fashion phases of Jackie, a magician notable only for performing magic tricks adequately while wearing a dress, and a tribute by a Filipino queen to the legend of Imelda Marcos (including a frightening rendition of "*Peelings*"). While none of this would have held much appeal for our intrepid pair (okay, the Jackie tableaux would have been something to see), it certainly would have been much better than the aural assault perpetrated on them by the disc jockey.

Unspeakably painful grunge music filled the bar as Binky and Doan rolled their eyes at each other. "There's no way you're talking me out of ordering room service after this evening," she said. "I'll deserve all kinds of unadulterated joy after this."

"If I take the phone out of your hand this time," Doan answered, "it'll only be to double the order."

They ordered four martinis. Each chugged one down to kill the pain in their ears, then they carried the other dose of sedative to the corner of the room farthest from the speakers.

"Well, for once you can't complain that I'm taking the good ones," Binky noted.

"Hmph," Doan noted wearily. "These boys are looking for their mirror images, dear. Either that, or they're attracted to real, freaky drag queens, not the amazing verisimilitude of womanhood that is *moi*."

"Well, that guy over there at the bar is looking at you," Binky countered.

Their corner position gave them a good line of sight down the bar. Doan scanned the patrons frantically waving at the bartender to get in their orders for shots of Jägermeister, and he did indeed find one man looking his way rather than at himself in the mirror behind the bar. With a gay man's instantly calculating faculties, Doan summed him up. He was young, probably midtwenties (too young for Doan), with a Mossimo baseball cap, a baggy Charlie Brown shirt over baggy, waist-below-the-ass jeans, some scraggly facial hair on his chin, and a pierced eyebrow. Yet there was no disguising the face: For all the accoutrements of the underclass around it, that face's pure patrician beauty shone through. It was like putting a Ralph Lauren model in a Diesel ad; birth and breeding and class were not to be subsumed by mere fashion. Even Binky noticed it, having grown up in Connecticut among such firm jawlines, tight narrow lips, and clear blue eyes.

"Here he comes," Binky whispered. "Should I leave the two of you alone?"

"Not yet," Doan said strategically.

The young man approached them, beer in hand. "Are you Binky and Doan?"

"We sure are," Doan said, kicking himself for not having realized that this must be their informer. "And you are . . . ?"

He held out a hand. "Tyler Anderson. Here, let's go where we can talk." He led them to the back, past the bathrooms. A man stood at a door with a glitter-coated star taped on it; a quick hello and kiss from Tyler and the door was opened for them.

"Are you telling me a place this tiny has a VIP room?" Doan asked incredulously.

Tyler laughed. "Nah. This is the manager's office-slash–dressing room." The room was indeed both, a series of federal government desks and chairs tarted up with full-size lighted makeup mirrors plastered with pictures of famous women. "Have a seat."

They sat. "So," Binky began, "how did you know us? And how did you know we're working on the Jeff Breeze case? And who was that guy who gave us the note at the funeral?"

Tyler's lip curled. "Lotta questions. Guess you guys really are detectives after all."

Doan didn't argue with that. "It's not that we're not grateful for any help you can give us, we're just . . . a little in the dark as to why you know so much about us, when we don't know anything about you.''

"Well, it may surprise you to learn this, but L.A. is really basically a small town." In fact, this did not surprise them, since San Francisco was also basically a small town. "Word gets around fast, especially when it has anything to do with celebrities.''

Binky pressed her point. "So word is out that somebody isn't taking it for granted that Kenny Wells killed Jeff Breeze. How did you get from that to us?''

Tyler smiled. "I can't really say who my source is. Let's just say it's someone else who also knows that Kenny Wells didn't kill Jeff Breeze.''

Binky and Doan couldn't help exchanging significant looks. "You look surprised,'' Tyler noted.

"I suppose we've gotten used to thinking we're the only ones who believe Kenny's story,'' Doan said.

"There are a lot of people who wanted to see Jeff Breeze dead. And some who needed to see him dead.''

"What do you mean?'' Binky asked.

Tyler stood up. "Do you want another drink? The bartender's my ex-boyfriend, so they're on the house.'' Neither of his guests could resist, and he left them to chew impatiently on what he'd meant.

"Honey . . .'' Doan started.

"Yes, dear?''

"There's really only a few people who know what we're doing down here. Luke, Eleanor, Kenny . . . and Sam Braverman.''

"Are you saying Sam Braverman tipped off our new friend?''

"No, I'm not. I mean, why would he? He was there when Breeze got killed. He's got every reason to believe that Kenny did it. Why would he assist us by giving us a source? Unless he's that eager to get in your pants.''

Binky frowned. "No, he could get in my pants with less trouble than that.'' Doan raised an eyebrow, but allowed her to continue without comment. "Kenny said Sam's a fixer, right? That he knows all the secrets in this town, and keeps them secret. Maybe he knows something we don't. That wouldn't be hard," she said, demoralized at their lack of information.

Doan patted her knee. "There, there. After all, we've only been here one day, and look! We've gotten into the funeral, seen the important people in Breeze's life, and now we've got a source. Well, maybe," he hesitated. "This guy could be scamming us." He grew indignant. "Sam Braverman might even have sent him to throw us off the trail!"

"Let's not be hasty," Binky said, in no hurry to damn her latest infatuation. "Let's wait for Tyler to tell us what he brought us here to tell us."

Tyler returned with a tray of drinks, which he presented with a flourish. "Tips are gladly accepted," he smiled.

Doan and Binky took some liquid restorative before pressing on. "So how did you know we were on this case?" Binky asked.

"I can't really tell you."

"Do you know Sam Braverman?" Doan asked.

Tyler smiled. "Everybody knows Sam, if only by reputation."

"That's not the answer I was looking for," Doan said. "Okay. Who was the guy at the funeral who gave us the note?"

"A middleman."

Doan sighed. "Listen. You brought us here to tell us something, I assume, but you're not saying anything. Should we thank you for the drink and leave?"

Tyler sighed, his smile fading. "I can't tell you who put me in touch with you. But I can tell you why I want you to find Jeff's killer."

They waited, respectful of the pregnant pause that often preceded exciting news.

''As the tabloids would put it, I was Jeff Breeze's 'gay lover.' ''

SIX

*N*either Doan nor Binky was one for gasping, but on this occasion they shared arched eyebrows as they regarded this bombshell. "So he *was* gay! Kenny will be so happy to hear it," Doan said.

Binky was a little less trusting of the face value of such proclamations. "I don't mean to impugn your integrity, but how do we know you're telling the truth?"

Tyler smiled. "You mean, do I have photos of me and Jeff cuddling for the camera? No. Jeff would never be photographed with me—he used to joke about my selling him out to the *Enquirer*. But if you can get to her, you can ask Jennifer Breeze."

"She knew about the two of you?" Doan asked, eager for more details of this unlikely ménage à trois.

"She could just deny it, even if it were true," Binky said thoughtfully. "After all, she spent so much time in that *Pendennis* interview—the one Cory Kissell did with the two of them—talking about how much she loved Jeff and how great the sex was, blah blah blah."

"You've been doing your homework!" Doan said admiringly. Binky chose to accept the compliment rather than acknowledge that reading trashy magazines was just the kind of homework for which she was most constitutionally suited.

"Mary Duveen engineered that marriage," Tyler said. "The rumors were starting to come out that Jeff was gay."

"The summer on Fire Island at Reid's house!" Doan said, recalling in a flash. "That story must have started circulating right before they got married."

"So Mary picked one of her other clients, someone she thought would trade a normal married life for a shot at movie superstardom. To wit, Jennifer Breeze, née Lane. God, was that a stroke of genius! After she and Jennifer made the deal, she got Jennifer a bit part in *Soldier Boy*, which picture, I'm sure you know, got Jeff his first Oscar nomination."

"I loved that movie," Doan whispered. "Jeff Breeze in uniform—a dream!"

"Then they started 'dating,' getting seen and photographed around town. Hollywood hasn't seen the likes of it since the old studio system days. Meanwhile, Mary Duveen plants stories in *Pendennis* and *People* and all those rags, all about 'Jeff in love!' the public eats it up, the gay rumors disappear, they get married in a huge ceremony at the Church of Dollars, adopt kids, and live happily ever after," Tyler concluded with a scowl.

"How does Mary Duveen get the magazines to run these stories?" Binky asked.

"She keeps the entire entertainment media in this town under her thumb. You don't get an interview with Jeff Breeze, or Charlotte Kane, or Ted Trask, unless you put them on the cover, submit the questions in advance, and give them the opportunity to 'correct' their answers before the piece runs."

"Ah, journalistic ethics!" Doan sighed.

"Those mags don't really care about ethics, they care about selling more copies. Put Jeff Breeze on the cover, you sell more copies. Editors not willing to run Mary Duveen's gauntlet and kowtow to her don't get interviews with her stars.''

"So where do you come into all this?" Binky asked.

Tyler sighed. "I met Jeff on the set of *Soldier Boy*. I had a bit part—one of the first guys to get killed.''

"Like the security guards on the old *Star Trek*!" Doan enthused. "You always knew when they beamed down to a planet and it was Kirk and Spock and Sulu and Bones and some nobody in a red shirt, that the nobody was going to get killed, so Bones could say, 'He's dead, Jim,' right before the crescendo!"

"As you were saying," Binky said, casting Doan a reproving glance. "So you're an actor."

"Yeah. I mean, in the usual way. Model-actor, waiter-actor, unemployed actor. Basically, I've always been the 'He's dead, Jim' character.''

"Did Mary Duveen know about your relationship with Jeff?" Binky asked.

He smiled. "Sure she did. She knows everything. Sam Braverman works for her, after all.''

"Sam Braverman seems to work for everyone," Binky noted.

"She laid down the law to Jeff: no gay bars, no sex clubs, no gay events, no AIDS benefits, no nothing that could remotely tie him to faggotry. She even vetoed his appearance at a pediatric AIDS fund-raiser!''

"Why do you sound so surprised?" Doan asked.

"Because pediatric AIDS has been the favorite charity of closeted gay stars for years. They try to take the heat off from the gay press about their being closeted by doing 'something for AIDS' but they make sure it's something that's not for the junkies and faggots. Bad publicity, you know," he finished bitterly.

"So the two of you met on the set of *Soldier Boy* at the same time he allegedly met and fell madly in love with Jennifer Lane. The irony!" Doan said with delight.

"Except he really fell in love with me."

"If you're an actor, and Mary Duveen has so much power, didn't she threaten you with expulsion from the industry if you took up with Jeff?" Binky asked.

"To get Jeff to get married, she needed to cut a deal with him, too. She knew he had to have sex, and she preferred that it be with someone in the industry, someone she could control. She laid down the law to us: We could only meet at Jeff's house, we couldn't go out in public together, we couldn't be photographed together, not even a personal Polaroid."

Doan shuddered. "No dating, just sex. Doesn't sound like much fun," he said, being the kind of guy who liked being amused by a man out of bed as much as if not more than he enjoyed the in-bed entertainment.

Tyler laughed. "Well, the sex was great, believe me. Maybe because it was so clandestine, so forbidden." At this, Doan thought of but chose not to mention the penile implant found during the autopsy.

"But *Soldier Boy* was six years ago," Binky said. "You mean the two of you had a completely clandestine relationship for *six years?*"

"Yep."

"And Jennifer Breeze knew all about it."

"Sure she did. She knew what she was getting into when she signed on. She gives up a chance at love in exchange for an incredible jolt to her career. One day she's just another C-list player, the next she's a star."

"Is she talented?" Doan asked.

"Depends on who you ask," Tyler said. "Fact is, some studios hire her for big parts just because they want to stay on Jeff's—and Mary's—good side."

Binky came at last to the sixty-four-thousand-dollar question. "So tell us. Who did kill Jeff Breeze?"

Tyler sighed. "I don't know."

"Well!" Doan huffed. "Then that note was the world's biggest bait and switch, wasn't it?"

Tyler stood up. "Can I get you another drink? I can tell you the names of the people who'd want Jeff dead, and why. Then you can figure out which one did it."

"What makes you think Kenny Wells didn't do it after all?" Binky asked.

"Because a lot of people wanted Jeff dead all of a sudden."

"Why?"

"Because Jeff and I had talked. A lot. About being in the closet. About the life we were—or weren't—leading together. You see, we'd decided to come out of the closet together. Jeff was going to leave Jennifer, and Mary Duveen, and Hollywood. For me."

Binky and Doan traded glances, in which they made a silent compact. They had already dropped their jaws like bumpkins once that evening, and once was enough; a little sangfroid in the face of any further bombshells was felt to be best. Doan immediately pulled the illustrated list out of his pocket. "Let me guess. Some of those people would be right here, no?" He handed the list to Tyler.

"Yep. That about covers it. Most everybody on this list had a motive. Jennifer Breeze would have been publicly humiliated if Jeff had revealed that their marriage was a sham. So humiliated she would have had to leave town."

"Well," Binky said, "that is the kind of story that makes Hugh Grant look like a little angel for merely consorting with hookers."

"But she's still going to get all Jeff's money," Doan noted. "I mean, she doesn't need a career."

"Things are different down here," Tyler noted. "Money isn't so important." At his audience's raised eyebrows, he elaborated. "I mean, when you're at that level, everybody's got plenty of money. Once you pass a certain amount in your bank account, it becomes about power. You're nobody, and you think all you need is money. Then you get money, and you forget that that was all you wanted; now you want power. You get off on the people kowtowing to you, you get off on the flashbulbs everywhere you go. You get a circle of dependents who flatter you all the time, who hate the people you hate, love who you love, and so on. Sure, she'll have plenty of money. But if the truth were to come out, she'd lose the life she's really come to love. And being all alone with your money is not anybody's idea of a good time here."

"Okay, what about Cory Kissell?" Binky asked.

"I doubt it. He's just Mary's flunkie. Of course, he'd have lost a lot of journalistic credibility when Jeff and I came out, but he could just say 'they lied to me.' Besides, *Pendennis* isn't too worried about credibility in their star bios."

"Ronald Piebald?" Doan asked.

"That's a possibility. Jeff Breeze was the poster boy for the Church of Dollars, after all. Bad PR for him would have been bad PR for the church. And as you might have figured out, the Church of Dollars isn't the type of institution to recoil from ruthlessness. But I'll tell you who the most likely suspect is: Mary Duveen." He paused.

"I'll bite," Binky said. "Why?"

"Jeff wasn't the only gay client on her roster. If he came out, the whole empire she's built could come crumbling down. I mean, everybody in the entertainment press in this town knows who's gay, and they know that Mary keeps the lid on that info. But if Jeff were to come out and let the world know that his whole life was a lie constructed by Mary Duveen, well, the truth about all her other clients might come out as well. Mary would be in the same situation as Jennifer Breeze: she'd still have the money she's piled up, but she'd lose all the incredible power she'd gotten used to."

"And who would she use to kill him?" Binky asked,

afraid of what the answer might do to her potential sex life.

"Sam Braverman," Tyler said with satisfaction. "He's done everything else—wiretapping, blackmail, bribery, anything to keep his clients' secrets. I don't see why a drastic situation wouldn't call for an equally drastic response."

"Or," Doan added helpfully, "it could be one of those other closeted stars in Mary Duveen's stable. After all, if it all comes down, it takes them with it, too, doesn't it?"

Binky was overwhelmed. "So many suspects . . ."

"So many people felt jeopardized," said Tyler.

Doan pondered this a moment then said, "Kenny Wells said something to me once about what happens when a gay star dies. He called it 'Now It Can Be Told' syndrome. You know, like River Phoenix. The general public never suspected a thing until he dropped dead. Then, next thing you know, a long article in *Premiere* about all the bisexuality and drugs. So won't it all come out sooner or later about Jeff Breeze, too?"

Tyler sighed. "That depends on me, I guess. You have to understand that stars live in a bubble. They don't go to the market, they don't go to Supercuts, they don't hang out at the corner bar. The only people they know are other stars, their entourages, and, if they're lucky, people who were their real friends before they became famous. Jeff used to complain that he didn't know any real people. He was like the prince in the tower, really: every luxury but freedom." He drifted off sadly for a moment, then came back. "The point being, nobody knew about Jeff wanting to come out but me, his wife, Mary, and probably Sam Braverman. And Jennifer, Sam, and Mary aren't talking."

"Are you going to talk? I mean to the press," Binky asked.

"I don't know. Part of me wants to blow the whole

lot of them sky high. And part of me says to let Jeff rest
in peace. A lot of people out there in the world loved
him, maybe for the wrong reasons, and a lot of them
fantasized that someday Jeff would come to their town
and fall in love with them and carry them off. And it
doesn't really matter, now, does it? He's dead.'' His
eyes brimmed with tears, as if this was something he'd
forgotten earlier and only now remembered.

Binky and Doan were not usually the comforting
types, but their trip to the Church of Dollars had
plumbed the depths of their selfishness. They both
moved to embrace him.

"Listen,'' Doan said. "If you do go public, maybe
everybody gets punished who deserves to be for making
Jeff live a lie. But maybe the person who killed him gets
away in all the confusion. Let us see what we can do,
okay? Before you go to the press.''

Tyler laughed between sobs. "And who's going to
believe me? When I don't even have a photo of Jeff to
prove I'm not lying?''

Doan and Binky looked at each other. "We'll find
something,'' Binky promised. "Trust us?''

"Do I have a choice?'' Tyler asked.

"Not really,'' Doan admitted. "But I'll tell you something: Sam Braverman and Mary Duveen aren't the only
characters in this story capable of a little dissimulation
in order to get their way.''

Back at the hotel, they passed on cocktails in exchange
for black coffee. "This is really depressing,'' Doan said,
and Binky didn't disagree. Living in San Francisco,
where homosexuals comprised upwards of 20 percent of
the population, they had gotten used to a world where a
deviant sexual orientation was not only not concealed,
but advertised at every opportunity. The writer Armi-
stead Maupin once observed that "in this town, the love
that dare not speak its name, never shuts up.'' In Hol-

lywood, homosexuality was viewed about as it was in, say, Peoria. Not surprisingly, considering that Hollywood's goods had to make the shelves in all number of states as famous for the intolerance they did not advertise as they were for the vegetables they trumpeted.

Even more depressing was the realization that a quick jaunt to L.A. was not going to solve this case. It was one thing to charge a couple of nights at the Beverly Hills Hotel; quite another to make an extended stay of it, especially without a paying client. And an extended stay was obviously what was going to be required here.

"So," Binky said, "what are we going to do? I mean, what can we do?"

"Well . . ." Doan said.

Binky's alarms went off. "I know that tone, Doan. What is it you're hiding from me?"

"I'm not *hiding* anything. I just wanted to wait until you'd gotten a little rest before telling you. When you went to get the car, I confessed to Tyler that we couldn't afford to stay down here indefinitely. Well, it turns out he's leaving town for a while, to clear his head and get over Jeff's death. So," he concluded brightly, "he says we can stay in his apartment, at least for the next month!"

Binky pondered this. "What do we do about a car? We can't rent the one we've got forever."

"Also solved. Tyler will be flying out, so his car is your car."

"Does he know I don't have a driver's license?"

"Oops! It slipped my mind."

"I'll bet it did," Binky said reprovingly. "Anything else?"

"Well, yes, actually. Seems we've acquired an entrée into the kingdom of Mary Duveen. Tyler says she's looking for an assistant, so . . ."

"No," she said, standing up to emphasize her point.

"Oh, come on. Don't think of it as work; think of it as going undercover!"

"Doan, the whole reason I went into this detective thing with you was so that I wouldn't have to work at some goddamn office job. And now you want me to do just that!"

"It won't be forever," Doan consoled her. "Just long enough to snoop through her files and find out what she's hiding."

"Great. I not only have to be a secretary, I have to commit a felony."

"Is it a felony to look through the files you're in charge of keeping?"

"It's probably a felony to use what's in those files to get your boss accused of a crime, especially if she's not guilty. Besides, what are *you* going to do while I'm slaving away at some fluorescent-lit hellhole for some Type-A maniac?"

Doan shrugged. "I'll be out networking. Digging up clues. Tyler left me a list of people I should contact."

"Great. I could do that. Why don't *you* work for Mary Duveen?"

"Moi? I'm afraid these fingers have never walked across a keyboard, dearie. I'd be completely lost in an office."

"This sucks," she said bitterly.

"Just don't think of it as a job. I mean, think of it as a job enough so you don't get fired, but remember that this is just another step on the road to never having to work at such a job ever again. Besides," he added, "there's one last thing I was going to use to persuade you if my other charms didn't work."

Binky waited.

"You see, darling, you are going to be paid very well for our services. Tyler has friends at Mary Duveen's PR firm—which is how he knew about the job—and he says Mary pays her assistants about *fifty grand a year.*"

Binky's eyes immediately lit up. Fifty grand a year! Why, in addition to her thirty grand a year from her trust fund, that was . . . a lot! Enough to lift her out of the urban lower middle class. Doan didn't hesitate; he picked up the phone and ordered a celebratory bottle of champagne. A contented smile came over her face; she lulled in the soft fluffy contentment that comes from having plenty of ready cash. They remained in a quiet reverie until room service had made its sweet delivery.

"Ahh, sweet money!" Binky sighed.

"Think of it," Doan said, raising his glass. "Being able to buy the *full line* of Aveda hair and skin products."

"Unlimited M.A.C. cosmetics," she offered.

"Wodehouse first editions."

"Armani sunglasses."

"Armani *socks!*"

"Fresh-cut flowers all the time."

"And not just daisies—tulips! irises! weird tropical penis-looking thingies!"

"Ahhh," they chorused together.

"See!" Doan said. "Work won't be so bad. The difference is, you'll finally be paid what you're worth."

"You know," Binky said, pleasantly contemplating the bubbles in her glass, "this detective thing isn't such a bad gig after all."

"Amen!" Doan added. "And cheers!"

They clinked glasses, toasting the days of ease to come.

The next evening found the twosome meeting Tyler at his apartment complex. The 1960s building was in the heart of West Hollywood, only blocks away from Santa Monica Boulevard. A quick reconnaissance of the neighborhood had found a supermarket, a liquor store, a Starbucks, and an endless series of restaurants with outdoor seating. Ah, civilization!

Tyler's building looked dreary from the outside, despite the palm trees and overlush vegetation that seems oddly out of place in such a dry climate. Once inside, however, they found that the apartment looked out over a courtyard replete with swimming pool. "It's just like *Melrose Place!*" Doan enthused.

"Where do you think they got the idea?" Tyler asked. "Hollywood's full of buildings like this."

"Well, I love it," Doan said. "I can't wait to go swimming!" Binky bristled at the thought of Doan lying poolside while she slaved away indoors, but bit her tongue.

Tyler picked up his bags. "Okay, I'm off. Here's the number at my mom's if the building burns down or you get arrested or something, and here's the keys to the apartment and the car. This little one opens the parking garage."

At the door of the apartment they waved him off cheerfully. "Bye! Have fun!"

"How convenient," Doan said as the door closed behind Tyler, "that he can even return the rental car for us. Everything is working out wonderfully!"

"Hmm," Binky said noncommittally, taking a look around the apartment. "Doan," she called out from the bedroom.

"Yes, dear?"

"There appears to be one bedroom. And one bed."

"Oh." Doan's face fell. He eyed the couch ruefully. "And I suppose you want the bed."

"If I have to work," she said triumphantly, "I get the bedroom."

Doan didn't argue. "Okay, okay. Just let me have one of the pillows."

They made a pot of coffee and started to unpack.

Doan soon found himself snooping through Tyler's video collection.

"That's private property," Binky said. "Of our host."

"I'm just looking for some entertainment," he exonerated himself. "Oh my god."

"What?"

He indicated the cabinet beneath the TV. "This is just about the biggest collection of gay porn I've ever seen. Oh, get a load of these!" Binky came over and got an eyeful. None of the graphic outtakes depicted on the back covers fazed her in the least; no, her sensibility was offended not by the product but by the package.

"Oh, please," she said. " 'Giant'? 'Hot Beef Injection'? 'See Dick Cum'? *'Waiting to Impale'?!*"

"I can offer no apology for my people," Doan said without hesitation. "We are guilty, guilty, guilty."

"I don't get it. Here's a guy who's been getting laid on a regular basis for six years. What does he need with porno?"

Doan shrugged. It would simply have taken too much time and energy to explain the gay male libido. "And," Binky continued, "can you tell me why Tyler has a picture of himself in the bathroom?"

"That I can do," Doan said. "Most gay men have a picture of themselves on their wall. You see, we're so insecure that when we look in the mirror, we can always convince ourselves that we look terrible. But if you can take just one good photo, why, there's proof that you're not the dog you think you are! And some of us need to be reminded of that every day," he concluded.

"I feel so naive." She opened the refrigerator. "And the kitchen is bare. What are we going to do for dinner?"

"We'll do exactly what we do at home." Doan opened a drawer in the kitchen and removed a sheaf of menus with a flourish. "Behold!"

"I thought we were staying here to economize," she said darkly. "I don't want my hard-earned paychecks being consumed on takeout."

"We *are* economizing," Doan insisted. "Why, for the price of a single bottle of room service champagne at the Beverly Hills Hotel, we can have a scrumptious dinner delivered two or three times! Besides, which one of us would cook? I swore off cooking when I left KC. Do you cook?"

"Have you ever seen me cook?"

"No, but then I've never lived with you before. Think of it—we're roomies!" he said excitedly. Binky felt a nagging suspicion that sharing an apartment with Doan might be more like sharing a cell than having a slumber party, but decided not to say anything. "Besides, we're on a case. We can charge dinner—it's a business expense!"

"Right. With no client to pay the bill when it comes."

"Must you be so negative?"

Their first spat was interrupted by the ringing of the doorbell. They looked at each other. "Are you expecting anyone?"

"No. Are you?"

Doan opened the door. "Oh, hi!" said the dreadlocked man at the threshold. "You must be Binky and Doan. What strange names. I can't figure out which one of you is which."

"I'm Binky."

"I'm Doan."

The man extended a hand. "Nice to meet you. I'm Oblique."

"You seem pretty clear to me," Doan said.

"No!" He laughed. "That's my name. I'm a performance artist. I'm black. . . . I'm not transparent. . . . I'm oblique . . . Get it?"

"Ah," Binky said noncommittally, her experience with performance artists being that they were rarely good at any one thing, and thus settled for being mediocre at several.

"Tyler asked me to check in on you. He says I might be able to help you."

Doan remembered his manners. "Do come in."

"Thanks."

"So you know . . . the whole story?" Binky asked.

"You mean about Jeff and Tyler? And you guys are detectives? Sure. Don't worry, I'm the soul of discretion. You have to be in my line of work."

"A discreet performance artist? You must not get many grants," Doan said sympathetically.

"No, no. An artist is what I *am*. Hairstyling is what I *do*. I work for Monstro Pictures. Maybe you've seen my name in the credits—I did hair for *Teen Hookers II* . . . ? *Grandma's Axe III* . . . ? *Total Carnage* . . . ?" This last jogged Binky's memory.

"Sure. Jeff Breeze's last movie."

"He had great hair." Oblique sighed. "Real moviestar quality—never a bad hair day for Jeff. Oh, are you ordering in? Well, I can help you right away!" He took the menus out of Doan's hand and looked through them. "No. Too greasy. Too slow. No, this guy yells at you in Chinese if you don't give him a big tip. Yes. Yes. Yes. Okay. No."

"Thank you."

"Glad to help anybody who's going to get Kenny Wells off."

"Do you know Kenny?" Doan asked.

"No, but I read his column. Omigod, everybody reads it down here, from studio heads to drudges like me. The gay papers here are too chickenshit to write about gay Hollywood, so we have to import our news from San Francisco. Sometimes he even prints things I didn't know!"

"So you know a lot," Binky said. "Do you know Ted Trask and Charlotte Kane?"

"Fer sure. They're both so queer it hurts. So're Jamie Lyons, Bill Glaser, Helen Garrett . . ."

"I knew about Helen Garrett," Doan said. "When she was still a stand-up comic? Before her sitcom deal? She was out of the closet, then. Kenny says her publicist used to call the *Watchtower* and pitch her to them as this lesbian comic. Lucky for her they never wrote the article! Then she got the TV deal and pow! I didn't know you could go *back in* the closet once you were out."

"Happens all the time, honey," Oblique said. "Just look at Norman Layne. Gay as as a goose on Broadway, then he does *Cage of Folly* for Paramount and it makes him a star. Now he 'doesn't discuss his sexuality.' As if! No, you want a list of every queen in Hollywood, you just see Oblique."

"Does that include nonperformer types?" Binky asked. "Studio moguls?"

"*Everybody,*" Oblique emphasized. "There are no secrets in this town; there are just things that don't get printed." He looked at his watch. "Look, I have to go. We're doing night shots for *Heads Will Roll III*. If you want dish, I'm always right down the hall—three-A. See ya!"

The door shut behind him. "A black, gay, male Valley girl," Binky marvelled. "Just when I thought I'd seen it all."

"A black, gay, male Valley girl hairdresser *performance artist,*" Doan amended. "I like it. He's the first, well, San Francisco–type person we've met down here. Why, it's going to be just like home!"

"We'll see about that," Binky said darkly.

SEVEN

❦

The next morning Binky found herself at the offices of Mary Duveen and Associates. She had expected a suite in some unremarkable urban tower; she had not expected to find the MDA Building, a free-standing monument to the ego of Mary Duveen. Designed in the 1980s, the MDA building came crashing down on the viewer with all the imperial excess of the age. This Babylonian pyramid of glittering black glass was terraced with narrow gardens overlush with exotic flowers that needed frequent and expensive replacement. Since, in the tradition of modern office buildings, the windows did not open to allow fresh air in or workers out to tend the gardens, it was necessary to install, as an afterthought to the completion of the building, small, narrow, nearly invisible black marble stairs along the four corners of the pyramid, to allow the multitude of on-staff gardeners access to the vegetation. And, in the tradition of pyramids everywhere, each year a few hapless workers plunged to their death down these slippery slopes.

Binky parked in the underground garage beneath the pyramid and took the elevator to the top floor, which took up about a fifth of the bulk of the pyramid. It certainly was magnificent; Binky paused where the elevator let her out, near the north wall. Gigantic single panes of smoked glass angled from the floor on three sides toward the cap of the pyramid, a black marble square suspending something resembling a giant shower head, which sent down a gentle spray of water into a shallow pool in the center of the floor. The view of the surrounding greater Los Angeles area was tremendous. The plants here were even larger and more exotic than those on the outside.

"May I help you?" a voice echoed in the chamber, just barely above the plashing of the water.

Binky looked around for the source, and found a reception desk on the other side of the waterfall. "I'm here to see Mary Duveen."

"Do you have an appointment?"

"I'm here about the assistant job."

The girl, equally beautiful as her surroundings, blinked, but that was all. "One moment." She pressed a button on her console and muttered softly.

Within seconds a great force entered the room. Mary Duveen was not a small person. She was nearly six feet, fat but not enormous. Her natural walk resembled the exaggerated steps of the power-walker—hips twisting madly, arms swinging slightly absurdly. She wore a khaki skirt high above her waist—nearly beneath her breasts. Her hair, cut in a sensible brown bob, obviously consumed a lot of expensive products to look so shiny and lustrous. Binky's practiced eye could tell Mary's hair would have looked the mousy type had it not been for the prodigious amount of money she had available for self-improvement. But Mary's most striking feature was her eyes. She was so nearsighted that the lenses of her round, black-framed glasses magnified her eyes to the size of skipping rocks. With those eyes on her,

Binky felt her secret mission would be extracted before she could make a dash to the elevator.

"Hi. I'm Mary Duveen."

"Nice to meet you. Binky Van de Kamp."

"Any relation to the Connecticut Van de Kamps?"

Binky was astonished. "Well, yes."

Mary laughed loudly. "Don't be so surprised! I know *everybody*. So you're here about the assistant job?"

"Yes."

"I just fired my last assistant three days ago." The eyes focused in on her. "How did you know there was a job?"

She shrugged. "You hear things. On the grapevine."

Mary laughed again. "Well, come back here, we'll talk."

She led Binky into an office on the other side of the floor's only wall. The view was even more magnificent than the one from the foyer, as it encompassed the splendid gardens and fountains arrayed in front of the pyramid. Mary sat behind her desk, a kidney-shaped slab of marble whose only resident was a phone.

"I'll tell you something," Mary whispered confidentially. "I liked your answer. I need somebody who's plugged into the grapevine." Binky did not see fit to tell Mary that reading *Movieline* was about as plugged into the grapevine as she'd ever been. "So tell me about your experience."

"Well, I've been a personal assistant to Eleanor Van Owens for several years now—"

"Right, Charles Ambermere's wronged wife. So, you're from San Francisco!" she said in the faintly patronizing way that those who are not from San Francisco often address those who are. "So what brings you to Hollywood?"

"Well, I enjoyed working for Eleanor, but my career really wasn't going anywhere."

"Say no more. I left a small town myself for bigger

pastures at your age!'' Binky bristled at the thought of
The City, as it was (admittedly pretentiously) called by
the natives, being compared to some burg in Iowherever.
''Are you impressed by famous people? Movie stars?''

''I'm afraid the only movie stars who impress me are
dead,'' Binky said, her first true statement of the conversation.

Mary roared with laughter. ''No, they sure don't make
'em like they used to!'' She sobered up. ''Let me tell
you a little about the job. I answer my own phone—''
As if on cue, her phone rang. ''Mary Duveen,'' she said
in flat tones, as if announcing her name to a maître d'.
''Who? I don't know you.'' She hung up. ''Most of
my calls are from my clients, either them or someone
involved with one of their projects—studio heads, et
cetera. I like to be directly available—it sets you apart
in this town. When I get a call from someone like
that''—she nodded toward the phone—''trying to sell
me something, I hang up. Let him go through chan-
nels!'' She laughed. ''I will give your number to people,
if for some reason they can't get ahold of me. Mostly
your job consists of talking to people either when I'm
too busy to talk to them or, more likely, when they're
not important enough for me to talk to. You screen anybody who I actually need to talk to. We put out a lot of
invitations to screenings and parties, but we have people
downstairs for all the stuffing and Xeroxing and faxing
and mailing. How's your handwriting?''

''Miss Porter's school,'' Binky said, for once without
blushing.

Mary's eyes widened ever further. ''Well! An accomplished young woman!'' She leaned forward, going back
into confidential mode. '' I ask because we hand-deliver
invitations to really important people, and I insist they
be addressed in a fine hand. Do you know how hard it
is to find a fine hand in Los Angeles?''

''It's a vanishing skill,'' Binky acknowledged.

"Now, you've probably heard I'm tough on assistants. I pile on a lot of work, but I suppose you've also heard that the rewards are good." Binky perked up at this, but Mary strayed from this near and dear subject, leaning back again. "I don't suppose I have to ask you if you're tough enough. When can you start?"

"Today, if you can provide a signing bonus."

"A what!" Mary roared, nearly popping out of her chair.

Binky held her ground. "A signing bonus. Two weeks' pay, paid to me today. I just moved here; I have a lot of expenses."

Mary howled with laughter. "That takes a lot of nerve! Do you know how many mailroom clerks in this town would give their left nut to work for me?"

"How many mailroom clerks turned assistants have you gone through like tissues in the last year?"

"Hmm. You know what? I like you." She stabbed her phone. "Alice, make up a check to Binky Van de Kamp for twenty-five hundred dollars. I want it by the end of the day." She stabbed the button again without waiting for a response. She stood up and extended her hand. "Kid, you've got a job."

To her absolute amazement, Binky found herself glad to be working for Mary Duveen. Why, this was the very high-profile, powerful job she'd imagined snagging when she'd first started looking for a job at the opening of our story—only better: What job could she be more qualified for than one that consisted of reading magazines and talking on the phone?

Yes, to her joy, her first assignment was to read a magazine. Mary explained that she was too busy to read *Daily Variety* and the *Hollywood Reporter* cover to cover, but that somebody had to read it for her and let her know if there was any really interesting news about her clients. *Daily Variety* was an eye-opener to Binky, who was used to being on the receiving end of the infotainment pipeline rather than the producing end. Just about every movie made was reviewed; what was so unusual to her about *DV*'s reviews was that each began with a boldfaced paragraph, a sort of executive summary of both the film's artistic merit and its financial prospects. "*Biker Angels VI*," one such review began, "is remarkable only for the nearly identical nature of its plot to those of sequels *III* and *IV*, but why mess with a winning combination? A fresh set of babe-a-licious b-girls complement the unremarkable hero and ensure *B.A. VI* will do just as well at the box office (not to mention on video) as its predecessors." Unlike the reviewers in papers across America, who took the Art they covered Quite Seriously, the cheeky writers of *Daily Variety* knew they were writing for a businessman's daily. Binky liked the refreshing honesty.

Then she had to call the editor of *Confidential*. Like *Pendennis, Confidential* was an old magazine revived for nostalgic times, but unlike *Pendennis*, *Confidential* often felt qualms about its role as purveyor of unadulterated industry PR to the masses. This meant the occasional hard-hitting piece about, for instance, the Church of Dollars or Michael Jackson. Mary had not explained the reason behind the call, but the demands Binky was to make were quite clear.

"Yes, this is Binky at Mary Duveen's office. I'm calling for Mary regarding a couple of things. First, I'm afraid we're going to have to disinvite you and any staff members from any premieres to which you've received invitations. Also, your interviews with Charlotte Kane and Marty Hower are canceled. And I believe you have somewhere around seven hundred photos sent to you in press kits; if you'll look on the back you'll find they're listed as property of MDA—we'll be needing all those back."

The editor was apoplectic. "I see. I see. I know what

this is about. We're being punished, aren't we?''

"It sounds that way," Binky willingly admitted.

"Because Mary Duveen"—he spat the name—"is afraid of Tim's piece. Isn't that right?"

"What piece is that?"

He spluttered. "What piece? *What piece!* Tim O'Neill's piece on the late, great, and *very gay* Jeff Breeze.'' Alarms sounded in Binky's head. *Tim O'Neill,* she wrote down quickly. "America is going to find out that Mary's creation was a forgery. His marriage was a forgery, all Mary's PR was a forgery—*is* a forgery! And she thinks she can bully us into dropping the piece! Well, you tell her from me that *Confidential* is going to run this piece, and when the dust clears, we'll see which one of us is left standing!" He hung up.

Binky was shaking, not from the vituperation the editor had poured in her ear but from the news. *Confidential* was going to do one of those Now It Can Be Told stories! She had to call Doan, but this would not be possible just yet. Binky's corner office was about one-fifth the size of Mary's and had two doors—one, closed, to the foyer, the other, open, to Mary's office. Mary spent all her time on the phone—more to the point, on the speakerphone. Her voice would rise and fall as it had during her interview with Binky, roaring, then falling into the confidential cadences that made the listener feel she was imparting some intimate secret, rather than just more spin from the mistress of spin. If Mary's phone wasn't ringing, Mary was calling someone. Binky feared the day that Mary would find herself with nobody to talk to, and decide to come out and create some interesting project for Binky to do.

Binky overheard Mary respond to the ring of her phone now. "Mary Duveen. Jennifer! How are you? . . . Well, you should get out of town for a while. Get away from the press. Go to Fisher Island! Oh, the kids, that's right. . . . What? Hold on." For the first time that day,

Mary got up and closed the door between her office and Binky's. Binky reasoned, correctly, that the caller must be Jennifer Breeze, and she conjectured that Mary might have plenty reasons not to let her new assistant hear their secrets.

She lunged for the phone to call Doan, but it rang just as she touched it. "MDA, this is Binky," she answered. She was supposed to append, "How may I help you?" but she'd decided to omit this when Mary wasn't listening.

"Now there's a familiar voice in the last place I'd expect to find it," Sam Braverman said silkily into her ear.

Binky's blood froze. Exposed! And so soon. Best to hang up, pack her bag, and fly out the door (stopping to pick up that $2,500 check, of course). "Don't worry," Sam assured her. "I think I know what you're up to, and your secret is safe with me."

"Why's that?" Binky asked, genuinely perplexed.

"You mean, since I work for Mary? I work for a lot of people. I have a lot of motivations for everything I do. What are you doing tonight?"

"Are you asking me out on a date, or are you ordering me out on a date?"

Sam laughed. "I won't tell Mary you're a private detective just because you don't want to have a drink with me. Do I look that desperate for female companionship?"

"Not in the least," Binky admitted. "Still, some people are excited by having a helpless female in their grasp."

"And are you now a helpless female?" Sam asked, plainly toying with her.

"Again, not in the least. Working for Mary isn't a requirement of this case. It's just . . . helpful, in more ways than one."

"If I know Mary, you'll get out of there around seven

tonight. Can I pick you up in front of the pyramid?''

"Fine," Binky said. "Now, what did you really call about?"

"Oh, I was trying to reach Mary, but her line is busy. Which, you should know, is a feature on her phone she can turn on and off. She's got seven lines, and they're never all 'busy.' She must be on the phone with someone important."

"Yes, she is."

Sam waited. "Come on, Binky. You scratch my back, . . ."

"It's Jennifer Breeze."

Sam chuckled. "Yeah, I can see how she might not want that conversation to be interrupted. Well, tell her I called, okay? And I'll see you tonight." He hung up.

She allowed her nerves a moment to settle before calling Doan, but she was interrupted again, this time by Mary, opening her door and yelling it at the same time. "God, that woman drives me crazy! You don't know any good nannies, do you?"

"Nannies?"

"For the Breeze kids. They've fired another one. I wish she could control those kids for *just one day*." Mary took a deep breath. "No matter." Then, desperate, she whispered, "It doesn't even have to be a licensed child care provider. Just someone who isn't going to molest them—though I pity the fool who tries anything on those creepy kids. In fact, it might be better if it were someone who *wasn't* a traditional nanny, since those are the ones the Breeze brats seem to drive crazy the fastest. They just need somebody who's used to . . . weird people."

A spark ignited behind Binky's eyes. "Weird people, eh? You know, I know someone who's looking for a job who might be just the right candidate. And," she added, barely able to suppress a smirk, "he can start right away."

Mary went off to a late power lunch and Binky finally had her opportunity to call Doan. "Hello?" he said, the stereo blaring Doris Day in the background.

"Why aren't you out detecting?" she asked accusingly. "Making those connections you were talking about?"

"It's too early! Everyone's just waking up from their late nights, going to the gym, deciding what to wear tonight. Where have you been all day?"

"At MDA. Mary Duveen hired me on the spot." She decided to withhold the news about the bonus, for now; she would have it spent fast enough without giving Doan time to think of even faster ways to make it evaporate.

Doan squealed. "That's my girl! I knew you were the one. So what's the salary?"

"Fifty grand, just as you said. Actually, it's not such a bad job," she said, unable to resist sticking the knife in. "All I do is talk on the phone and read magazines all day."

"Oh, my god, that's my *dream job!*" Doan moaned enviously. "So have you found out anything interesting?"

"A couple of things. Here's something you can do this afternoon. Call *Confidential* and ask for Tim O'Neill. He's writing a piece on Jeff Breeze and Mary Duveen is doing everything in her power to kill it."

"How exciting. Do you think he'll really spill anything to me? I mean, writers have that unpleasant tendency not to dish out juicy gossip before it appears under their bylines."

"Use your charms. If I can charm Mary Duveen, you can charm some infotainment reporter. Oh," she said casually, "and something else. You have a job interview tomorrow."

"What?!"

"Yes. You're applying for the position of nanny to the widow Breeze's two adopted children."

Doan spluttered disbelievingly. "What are you talking about! Me? Kids? Listen, honey, it's one thing for you to do what you would have to do anyway if we didn't have a detective agency, but if the success of this agency depends on me changing diapers and chaperoning tots, we are *closed*."

"Calm down. There's a daughter who's sixteen, a son who's fourteen. Mary says they don't really need a nanny, it's just that Mamma Breeze isn't around them much—as little as she can be, I think—but she's worried about the tabloids labeling her a neglectful mother. So the little darlings just need someone on hand so Child Welfare doesn't come snooping around."

"Right, like Child Welfare has ever come 'snooping around' a famous person's house. Wait a minute—the Breezes were only married about six years, right? How'd they get kids so old?"

"Because, like you, dear, neither Breeze wanted anything to do with anything in diapers. Two astonishingly underprivileged children with astonishingly privileged bone structures were selected after an exhaustive talent search as the most decorative accessories to the Breezes' married life. Listen, just go to the interview. You're not being interviewed by Jennifer, she could care less who watches the kids—she lets them pick their own nannies." She decided not to warn Doan that the kids went through nannies like Mary Duveen went through assistants.

"They're probably really screwed-up kids, don't you think? I mean, having a pair of parents who don't love each other and don't love them?"

"Probably. Doan, you don't have to take the job. Just go to the interview and see what you can learn from the kids." Binky heard Doan sigh, which she knew was a sign he was giving in. Enough with the stick; time for the carrot. "A town car will pick you up and whisk you to the interview tomorrow at noon. Since the Breeze children aren't old enough to drive, anywhere you'd travel with them you'd go in the lap of chauffeured luxury.''

"Ahh, yes. Remember when *Pendennis* asked Fran Lebowitz her favorite name, and she said, 'Driver'? How true.'' He squirmed with delight at the thought of imminent luxury. "All right, I'll go."

"Good. And call Tim O'Neill this afternoon. Oh, and don't wait up for me."

Doan paused. "What do you mean?"

"I'm going out tonight."

"With Sam Braverman, I assume."

"Yes," she said defiantly.

"Fine," Doan said, to her surprise.

"You're not going to give me a lecture about Luke?"

"No," he said airily, "I've decided to let you get this out of your system. Maybe this will make you realize just how fantastic Luke really is."

"You're acting as if Sam were some kind of reptile."

"Well . . ." Doan began, "he *did* work for Jeff Breeze, and he *does* work for Mary Duveen, and he *is* the official secret keeper of Hollywood. Hey, you should ask him for the dish on Michael Jackson and O.J.—I bet he knows *everything*."

"And he let us into Jeff Breeze's funeral, and he called Mary Duveen today and got me instead and thought it was amusing."

"Oh my god, are you in danger? Is he going to tell Mary Duveen?"

"No. I don't think so. He's . . . he's got his own agenda in all of this. I mean, I really don't think he had anything to do with the murder. He's too interested in helping us find the killer."

"Or he's interested in making it *look* like he's interested in helping us find the killer, even as he leads us down blind alleys."

"Cynic."

"Dreamer."

"I have to go. I have to call and speak with Harrison Ford."

"Oh, you really know how to hurt me! I'm so jealous right now."

"Call Tim O'Neill. I'm sure he knows plenty of famous people."

Sam, Binky thought, was full of surprises. In an Armani town, Sam seemed to live in Brooks Brothers. He pulled up in front of the MDA pyramid in a new Acura Legend—luxurious, a bit pricey, but hardly a heavy-duty status symbol vehicle in a town where you are what you drive. Understated, that seemed to be the word for Sam Braverman. He was used to working with people with bigger egos and greater insecurity than he could ever match, and was content to take the copilot's seat in the drama. She watched his wry smile as they drove down Sunset, and she wondered what he thought of the people he worked for.

The restaurant he took her to was telling, too—not Spago or Mortons or anywhere even close, but a cute little Italian place on Santa Monica Boulevard, in the heart of the gay neighborhood, just blocks from Tyler's apartment. Whereas in San Francisco outdoor seating was generally confined to the rear of restaurants, in a see-and-be-seen town like this the outdoor seating was located in the front, along the sidewalk, where everyone could see you dripping tomato sauce down your front— which was probably why all the other patrons were drinking but not eating.

"So what did you do before you were . . . whatever it is you are now?"

"Well, I grew up in Israel. I was in Israeli security for about ten years."

"Oh, doing what?"

"Ever hear of the Mossad?"

"No," Binky admitted.

"Well, that's what I did." He smiled.

"Thank you. How helpful. Now I have to start the conversation all over again. Most displeasing."

"It's the . . . well, the closest thing I can think of is that it's like the CIA and NSA sort of rolled into one."

"Ah. A spy."

"No. An intelligence gatherer. Sometimes called upon to act on that intelligence."

"I see. Good experience for this job, eh?"

Sam laughed. "This is a little less dangerous, but yes."

"So just what is it that you do? I mean, you were doing security for Jeff Breeze when we met, but you're not a bodyguard."

Sam checked the proferred bottle of wine and made a cursory gesture to the waiter to go ahead and pour. "I work in security. And that means a lot of things. Keeping people safe. Keeping secrets safe. It's a combination of PR agent, bodyguard, private investigator," he said, giving her a nod, "and attorney. In short, I defend people."

"From their enemies? Or from themselves?"

Sam sipped his wine and smiled. "Very good. Very good. Sometimes from themselves. Usually from those who'd exploit them or their private lives for personal gain."

"Be that blackmailers, vengeful ex-lovers, reporters . . . detectives."

"Usually."

"So you kept Jeff Breeze's secrets. You keep Mary Duveen's, one of which is that she engineered the marriage with Jennifer Breeze." Sam raised an eyebrow, impressed by her rapidly gained knowledge. "So why are you helping us blow the lid off your employers?"

"Is that what you're doing?"

"It looks that way. I mean—" She stopped, hesitant. She had been so blinded by lust for Sam (and so thoroughly charmed by him) that Doan's admonishment about hidden agendas had been a good thing. How much to tell Sam? Should she have even admitted she knew about the engineered marriage? Could he guess that she must also know about Tyler?—for surely *he* already knew about that.

Sam reached across the table and took her hand. "I have a proposal."

"I don't know, it's so sudden."

"No, no. I propose that tonight we don't talk about Mary Duveen, or Jeff Breeze, or Jennifer Breeze, or Hollywood. You don't know how much to trust me, and I don't yet know what to make of you. As a detective, that is. I've got a pretty good idea what to make of you as a woman."

Binky blushed. "That sounds like a plan."

Sam raised his glass. "Here's to a nice date between two acquaintances."

Binky clinked her glass against his. "Amen," she said, relieved that her day of detecting was finally over.

Doan was not the least bit surprised when Binky did not come home that night. In fact, he'd been so sure she wouldn't that he slept in the bed rather than on the couch. Every dark cloud, he reflected with satisfaction the next morning, stretching lazily in Tyler's comfy bed, had its silver lining; Binky may have thrown Luke over for someone Doan considered to be Luke's identical (albeit evil) twin, but every night she spent in sin with Sam Braverman would mean a good night's sleep for Doan.

He wasn't nervous about meeting Tim O'Neill for breakfast that morning, but he did take some few moments of agony over what to wear. The Anna Sui? No, too nightie-ish. That festive Todd Oldham dress? Nah, too East Village. He did want to be taken seriously; therefore, this was obviously a situation that called for

Donna Karan. It did not occur to him to wear men's clothes in order to be taken seriously.

His conversation with the *Confidential* writer the previous afternoon had been short but sweet. Revealing that he was a detective, he told O'Neill that he had some information that might be useful to his piece, and was willing to trade it for what O'Neill might know that could help him. The writer had readily agreed to meet him for breakfast the next morning at Musso and Frank's.

Musso and Frank's didn't look like any kind of industry hotbed; only the pile of copies of *Daily Variety* at the cash register indicated the crowd had anything to do with the movies. It struck Doan as a sort of Jewish Denny's, with sweet old waitresses who called you "hon" with a straight face and a menu featuring multifarious cheese blintzes. He took a seat in a padded plastic booth and waited for his contact.

Each had described himself only cursorily on the phone. "How will I know you?" Doan had asked.

"Well, I'm six-foot, dark curly hair, dark eyes, thirty-five. I'll be dressed casually. And you?"

"Oh, six-two, long blondish hair, thin, I'll have on something . . . dressy." He giggled.

"What?"

"Oh, it's just that it sounds like we're meeting for a blind date."

"Well, physically, you sound like someone I'd date."

"Yeah? That's funny, because I've got this thing about dark curly hair."

"Huh. Well, I guess we'll see tomorrow, eh? Maybe we'll end up on a date after all."

They laughed and hung up. Doan was now really looking forward to this liaison. There were some things he knew better than anybody, and chemistry was one of them. He'd had it plenty of times with men in the past, but to have chemistry *on the phone,* with someone he'd never even seen before, well, that was a new one.

Doan knew who Tim O'Neill was when he saw him, even though for one second he was sure it was too good to be true. The writer had been modest. He was closer to Doan's six-foot-two than the proffered six-even description. He did indeed have dark, curly hair, short and tight on top with the back and sides neatly trimmed. Doan could tell he had a killer body merely from the rippled forearms and half bicep popping out of his polo shirt, as well as the bulge of his pecs. There was no fat on this man; his quite simply magnificent jawline assured Doan of that. His dark eyes were all the more startling in his pale, ruggedly handsome face, a face shaded only by a bone structure–enhancing two days' worth of stubble. Doan spotted an easy sunburner in his new acquaintance and speculated that the looks came from Black Irish roots. In most men that good looking, the eyes were narrowed, a little squinty, looking about with disapproval at the inferior quality of the flesh around them, the lips pursed and the carriage stiff. But Tim's eyes, indeed his whole face, were wide open and welcoming, happy and curious; he walked with an easy swinging carriage. This was L.A., after all, so he knew he was gorgeous, but he didn't stand around looking at his watch, waiting for someone to notice.

And Tim knew who Doan was on sight, as well. Now, Doan McCandler had had his share of lovers over the years, but truth be told he was an acquired taste. It could not be said that he was feminine-looking, even though he could wear women's clothes and "pass," as it were, in most circles. No, he was more *feline* than anything. Most men attracted to men want, well, a man. A manly man. Doan certainly did, and he himself was anything but that. But he did possess a certain magnetism that often overcame men who thought they'd long ago settled on one specific type to be attracted to. He got up to shake Tim's big strong hand and knew the feeling was mutual.

"You underrated yourself on the phone," Doan said.

"See," Tim said, "if this *had* been a blind date, I would have lied and said I was six-foot-four, twenty-five instead of thirty-five, and 'very good-looking.' "

"The last of which would have been true," Doan replied.

"Thanks. I guess when you said 'dressy,' you were making a play on words."

"You never thought you'd meet a detective in a dress. Not a male one, anyway."

"When we were on the phone, after we talked about the blind date thing, I thought to myself, a gay detective, how interesting. I was looking forward to meeting you no matter what. And now . . ."

"And now?"

Tim smiled a killer smile and Doan felt his insides getting squishy. "Have you ordered?" Tim asked.

"Cheese blintzes seem to be the specialty of the house."

"Yeah, the strawberry ones are great."

They ordered and puttered with their coffee. "So you're writing a Now It Can Be Told piece about Jeff Breeze."

Tim laughed. "That phrase—I guess you read Kenny Wells's column."

Doan was still startled at how popular Kenny was in L.A., even though he was printed several hundred miles and a world away. "Kenny is actually my client."

Tim weighed this. "Huh. And you're looking to see who might have killed Jeff Breeze other than your client?"

"You are correct, sir."

"Any ideas?"

"A few."

Tim leaned forward, pitching his deep silky voice a

little lower. "Any you'd care to share?" Doan had already figured out that Tim was seducing him; he only had a moment's hesitation trying to figure out if it was Tim the man seducing Doan the man, or Tim the reporter seducing Doan the source. But unlike Binky's (probably wise) hesitancy about confessing all to Sam Braverman, Doan decided that, with a few choice exceptions, Tim could be told all the facts.

"A few names pop up, for various reasons. Mary Duveen. Jennifer Breeze. Sam Braverman, though only as button man for someone else. So what have you learned about Jeff Breeze?"

"Why would Jennifer Breeze want to kill her husband?" Tim asked in a tone that led Doan to believe he already knew why, and was testing Doan's actual knowledge of the case.

"Because if he left her for another man, as he was about to do, it would have humiliated her in front of the entire town. And left her without an income."

Tim's wide eyes grew perfectly circular. He was plainly astonished. "How do you know that?"

Doan smiled, glad to have the upper hand again after having lost it in the wave of lust that had rolled over him earlier. "My associate and I are in contact with the person with whom Jeff Breeze was going to . . . elope, as it were. We have every reason to believe him."

Tim shook his head. "I knew Breeze was gay, I knew there was a man on the side, but this— Can you hold on? I have to call my editor, it'll just take a second."

"Love 'em and leave 'em, eh?"

"No! No, no. It's just that we're about to go to press and . . . I don't want this article being printed without all the facts."

"Very conscientious of you. You may go," Doan indicated.

Tim was back by the time the blintzes arrived. "Sorry about that."

"Now, your punishment is to tell me what *you* know about Jeff Breeze."

Tim pushed back his plate in disgust. "I really hate this guy. I mean, he's dead and all that, and some people say we should let the dead lie, but when I look at his life I get so angry. And part of that is me, my past. I've always known I was gay. I told my parents I was gay when I was eighteen. I've always lived an open, gay life. And as a journalist, that's cost me a lot. I went to work in the gay press because when I got started, there was hardly a paper in the world that wanted someone on staff who wanted to write about gay issues and the gay community. Hell, even the *San Francisco Chronicle* only kept one or two token fags on the staff even through the eighties! And the only way out of the gay press was to move into the entertainment press. You know, I'm a good writer. I would like to be working for the *New York Times* right now. And I could be, if I'd been closeted early in my career, but I wouldn't live a lie. I'm not happy with where my career is right now, but I'm happy with who I am. Sure, I could have a lot more money—if I wanted to be a whore like Cory Kissell. And I look at Jeff Breeze, a gay man who never stopped hiding that fact—who not only hid it, but went to obscene lengths to eliminate even the *possible appearance* of the truth; I mean, it's one thing to go through with some sham marriage, but it's another to torture some kids with a loveless union just so you can be seen with them in public and keep commanding twelve million dollars a picture." He sighed, stopped, sipped his coffee. "I'm sorry. You asked me what I know about him, not how I feel about him."

"No, no, I totally understand. You might guess from looking at me that I've sacrificed certain things in order to be myself, too."

Tim laughed. "I guess you have!" He eyed Doan curiously, but it was a look Doan was used to from men—a look that said, basically, I can't believe I'm finding you attractive.

Doan broke their eyelock. "I guess it's my turn to eat and run." He hesitated only momentarily before looking into Tim's warm brown eyes and deciding to trust him. "I've got an interview with Jennifer Breeze this morning." As Tim's eyes widened, Doan added, "Not really an 'interview,' more like . . . a job interview. As the new Breeze nanny."

Tim threw back his head and laughed. "You won't get it."

"I don't expect to get it," Doan said huffily, "but what makes you so sure I won't?"

"You're out at breakfast with me, so you've been tagged. Somewhere in this restaurant—don't look around—is one of Sam Braverman's people. Really, don't bother, they're very good; I mean, none of them look remotely like cops or G-men. But they've been following me everywhere since I started this article. Mary Duveen's instructions. They'll start following you now, to find out who the hell you are."

Doan gulped nervously. "Following me?"

Tim smiled wickedly. "Don't worry. I can lose them."

EIGHT

~

Tim was as good as his word. Doan couldn't help
but think that while he may not have risen to the heights
of his profession, he'd made enough money to buy the
most darling little Alfa Romeo, and his fast, capable
driving, the look of his lean, hairy forearms grappling
with the gearshift, gave Doan no small sexual thrill.
Whatever pursuers they might have had were nowhere
to be seen by the time they got to Tyler's apartment.

"Well," Doan said, extending a hand, "it's been nice
meeting you."

Tim eyed him levelly. "Is that all?"

"No, there's also the fact that my insides get all quaky
when you look at me like that."

"Does that mean if I asked you out on a date, you'd
go?"

"Wild horses couldn't stop me," Doan replied, never
one to play games when exactly what he wanted offered
itself so easily.

Tim grinned. "Okay, then. I'd like to know what you
learn today as soon as possible. Though I'd like to see
you as soon as possible anyway."

"That can be arranged," Doan said. "Call me to-night." He wrote down Tyler's phone number and gave it to Tim. As he got out of the car, he said a little prayer that if Binky was going to take the wayward path away from Luke to Sam anyway, that she take it again tonight and leave the apartment in his sole possession.

Only minutes after Tim had dropped Doan off at the apartment, the Town Car arrived to whisk him to the Breeze compound. Doan realized that he'd had absolutely no opportunity to prepare for the interview, which gave him a momentary shudder of most un-Doan-like anxiety. But then, with a shrug, he simply acknowledged that there was no way he was going to get this job anyway, and it *would* be tantalizing to see the house of one of Hollywood's richest stars. Oh yes, and there might be clues to be found by talking to the Breeze children.

The car moved ever higher up the Hollywood hills. Doan thought there was something eerie about the whole area: every house was impressive, lush foliage nearly choking off the streets (there were no sidewalks); it would have all looked so serene, were it not for the sign in every single yard announcing menacingly that the house was protected by ARMED RESPONSE SECURITY. Doan remembered a Joan Didion book an old boyfriend had convinced him to read (a book that had convinced him never, ever to move to L.A.), and finally got the point of it.

The car took a turn around a hairpin curve and suddenly before him was a Famous Edifice. "It's Madonna's house!" he cried excitedly.

The driver turned around. "Not anymore. She moved, after her stalker found it. Too easy to get in."

Doan was surprised that the large black man had spoken. "I guess whoever buys it will repaint it," he said sadly, "and it'll be just another big pile."

"Whoever buys it will want to erase the evidence that

someone much more famous than themselves ever lived there.''

Doan laughed. "What's your name?"

"Charlie, sir."

"No 'sirs,' please. I'm Doan." They passed the rest of the trip in idle chatter. It turned out that Charlie had worked for the Breezes for years. Doan reflected that here was surely somebody who knew plenty of secrets about this household. He made a note to try and see what he could ask, inconspicuously, on the trip back.

There was nothing to suggest that one gated residence was any different from any other; certainly the one they pulled up to had no folksy wooden sign with "The Breezes" emblazoned on it. Charlie reached up and pressed a button over the rearview mirror and a gate swung open.

The house was unremarkable from the outside. It appeared to be simply a small, one-story edifice. Of course, Doan had done the same sort of homework as Binky had, though in his case it had been digging up an old copy of *In Style* with the usual fawning spread on the house and its inhabitants, so he knew that beyond the double front doors was the top floor of a five-story house that terraced the hillside. As soon as the car pulled up to the doors, they opened. Jennifer Breeze frowned as Doan got out.

"I don't have much time," she said by way of introducing herself. Doan looked at her and thought, She's not so hot. There were movie stars, such as Jennifer's late husband, who simply commanded the screen; you wanted to watch them no matter what they were doing. And then there were others, more manufactured and less durable, like Jennifer—attractive enough, talented enough, but not terribly *remarkable* in the way of real stars. Doan decided that Jennifer never would have been a star had it not been for her marriage.

"The kids are inside, so I'll leave you to them. I have

to go. Somebody will call you if you're hired.''

"You're not going to interview me?''

She looked at him coldly. "What for? Anybody I think is suitable, *they* just drive away.'' She gave him a sour little smile. "You're just fresh meat for the little beasts. Good luck.'' And with that, she got into the Town Car and was gone.

To say that Doan was easily appalled would be ludicrous. After all, he had lived in San Francisco for years, attending all manner of leather festivals and other bacchanals, and had seen just about everything under the sun that could shock. But Jennifer Breeze's open contempt for her own (admittedly adopted) children got Doan's sense of moral indignation going. If the children were in fact beasts, he reflected, such parents as this had surely made them so.

He walked into the silent and seemingly empty house. "Hello?'' he asked, the word echoing in the stillness. Realizing that Jennifer might not have informed her beasts that a potential new nanny was coming, he thought it best to try and find them. Using the photos from *In Style* in his head as a map, he began to look around.

The sitting room was exquisitely designed—for being photographed, that is, not for sitting in. There was no evidence of actual life in the room, and Doan "hmphed'' as he realized that the interesting and attractive books scattered around the room in the photo layout were nowhere to be seen.

Downstairs he found several master bedrooms (one for Jeff and one for Jennifer, of course, though Jennifer's separate quarters had been omitted from the *In Style* spread); a screening room, the most comfortable room in the whole house and probably the only one in which the residents spent much time; and the kitchen.

Getting nosy, Doan checked out the kitchen. Two full sets of copper pots and pans dangled from the ceiling over the freestanding cooking area with two ovens. Cooking utensils spilled out of attractive glass jars. One cabinet was stuffed with fine linen napkins and table-cloths. Doan found an ice cream machine, a bread maker, three blenders, a large and a small Cuisinart, a Mixmaster, a toaster, a bagel toaster, and a toaster oven. In the refrigerator was one yogurt and a bottle of Sto-lichnaya.

A throbbing base beat emanated from the lowest floor. When he got down there, he identified one room as the source of the music and another as the source of the clacking of a keyboard. Figuring that someone typing would probably be easier to deal with than someone playing Guns and Roses at . . . well, any volume, he moved toward the clacking.

He knocked on the open door. "Hello?"

The clacking stopped. "Who is it?" a girl's voice asked tensely.

"Um, my name's Doan. I'm here about the nanny position?"

"Oh." The voice was simultaneously disappointed and relieved (probably that it wasn't one of the multi-farious house-ravaging gangs that must surely have been the prompt for all those Armed Response signs). "Come in, I'll just log off."

Doan found the most amazingly beautiful sixteen-year-old blond girl sitting at the computer. And when she finished and turned toward him, he nearly gasped. That quality he had just been thinking about, and finding lacking, when looking at Jennifer Breeze, that *some-thingness* that made real stars, was present in this girl. She was like Dante's Beatrice, preternaturally calm and wise beyond her years.

"Writing your memoirs?" Doan asked.

She laughed, an easy, free laugh. "Maybe I oughta! No, just noodling around on the Internet. So I guess you

met Jennifer. Don't worry, you won't see much more of
her than that. We don't.''

"I see. She did stop long enough to tell me you'd be
the one picking your next nanny." He omitted the "little
beasts" remark. He extended a hand. "I'm Doan."

"Elise. Nice to meet you. And 'picking' isn't really
the word. Basically, you're hired. You'll quit soon
enough.''

"Why is that?" Doan asked.

Elise smiled serenely. "Because my brother is a ball
of flaming anger, and I'm really creepy.''

"Because you're so obviously wise beyond your
years?''

She looked at him for the first time as if she actually
saw somebody there. "I guess I am," she said.

"I think I can handle that.''

"So how long have you been a nanny?''

Doan looked into her cornflower blue eyes and
couldn't lie. "Well, I've never been a nanny, exactly.
Though it doesn't look like you need much looking after.''

"No," she admitted, "we don't. Just someone to
make sure we get fed and don't run away.''

"Sounds like a job for a jailer.''

She smiled. "That's about right.''

Doan was thoroughly depressed. "I need a drink," he
said with a sigh.

"There's a cabinet and fridge out by the pool. Here,
I'll show you." She led him out the sliding glass doors
from her room onto the patio. "I'm sure it's full. Jeff
and Jennifer never use the pool.''

Doan found all the makings for a Bombay Sapphire
martini and helped himself. He eyed Elise. "Normally
I'd say you're too young to drink, but in your case . . .''

She waved the offer away. "Thanks, but I'm clean
and sober.''

"I should hope so, at your age.''

She laughed. "I mean, I went through rehab when I was fourteen."

"Oh." He sipped guiltily at his drink. "So why aren't you in school?"

"We're in mourning for Jeff," she said lightly. "Two weeks off."

"Real close family."

"Being Jeff and Jennifer Breeze's kid isn't a family relation, it's a business arrangement." She shrugged. "Kevin and I both came out of the adoption-go-round, basically. We'd both knocked around foster homes, group homes, all that. I've learned to look at this arrangement as something I can use to improve my life. They can afford to send us to private school, which will get me into a good university, which they can also afford to send us to."

"Which they can't afford *not* to send you to." Seeing her questioning look, he explained. "I mean, you know, *la publicité,* if they didn't."

"Exactly."

Doan cast an eye toward the Breeze Junior's room. "And Kevin is using the situation to his benefit as well?"

"No. He basically just stays stoned all the time."

"That's how he copes with living in an unloving home, I suppose."

Elise narrowed her eyes in appraisal. "So what makes you want to be a nanny?"

Doan gulped. Lying had never come naturally to him. In fact, the reason he spent so much of his time in a dress was because wearing men's clothes had come to feel like a lie. San Francisco was, for all its faults, somewhere you could live without having to tell a lot of lies. He finished his drink and steeled himself.

"I'm not a nanny. I'm a private detective. A friend of mine has been accused of killing your father, and I think he's innocent. My partner is working undercover

in Mary Duveen's office; that's how I heard about this
job. I thought the interview might provide some clues.''

"And how else would you get to interview the Breeze
family?''

"Exactly. I'm sorry. I should be going.''

"Going where? The car's waiting for Jennifer to fin-
ish her Rolfing.''

"I'll walk. I'm really sorry.'' He started to go.

She held up a hand. "No. I want to hear more about
this. I didn't love Jeff, but I didn't hate him. I felt sorry
for him.''

"Because . . . ?''

She smiled a wicked, knowing, heartbreaking smile.
"If you're a detective, you must surely already know
that.''

"Because he was gay. Because he was in love with
another man, and had to hide it.''

"Hmm. You've been busy. Have you met the other
man?''

"Tyler?''

"The very same.''

Doan had trusted Tyler's word, but was nonetheless
relieved to get proof that their source had been telling
the truth. "Yes. I'm staying in his apartment right now,
as a matter of fact.''

She started to laugh, and couldn't stop. The absurdity
of the whole thing had her dancing around, giggling hysterically. Doan handed her a glass of water.

"I'm sorry. It's too funny.'' She sipped the water.
"Tyler was the only one who was ever nice to us. Well,
nice to me. Kevin never let him try.''

"So you saw a lot of him?''

"He and Jeff were here a lot. I mean, they couldn't
go anywhere else. This was their love nest. It's kind of
cute, I mean, it would be if it weren't so sad.''

"So you got to know Tyler pretty well?''

"Well, I wouldn't say that. I mean, better than I got

to know Jeff and Jennifer, that's for sure.''

"Would you say they were in love?"

She pondered this for a moment. "Yeah. I would."

"I guess I should tell you why Tyler thinks someone killed your father. He and Tyler were planning to run away together."

Elise's eyes widened in near disbelief. "Damn, this just gets better and better. They were really going to do it? He was really going to give it all up for love?" She stared thoughtfully into the pool. "I guess he wasn't so bad after all." Doan watched the wheels start to turn behind Elise's mask. She looked up at him. "Do you want to go shopping?"

"What?"

"Shopping. I'll call a car from the service and it'll take us shopping. We can spend some of the Breeze fortune—I've got lots of charge cards, which I've never used. Now seems like a good time."

"What about your brother?"

"Oh, he'll come along. We'll just have to find a video game arcade and park him there."

"Just one question. Why?"

"Why? I guess because I like you. I guess because you're the first person who hasn't lied to me since I arrived in this house."

Binky had described the Breeze children as astonishingly underprivileged children selected to be rescued from poverty thanks to their astonishingly privileged bone structures, and that was certainly the case. It was almost as if a decorator had picked the two of them—Elise so blond and golden, and Kevin so Heathcliff-like, with the dark brooding features of a future romance novel cover model. Kevin had grunted his assent to the trip in a manner that led Doan to believe that it was Elise who was responsible, or as responsible as she could be, for raising this boy.

They piled into the back of the hired town car. Kevin pulled out a joint and lit up. "Open the window," Elise told him. He shrugged and pushed the appropriate button. He took a toke and offered it to Doan.

"No thanks, I've found it doesn't really go with gin."

The car took them to the Galleria. After depositing Kevin in an arcade, Elise was not sparing with the platinum card. She bought and bought, mostly for Doan, who demurred at first and then, unable to contain his acquisitive nature (his conscience dulled by the fact of the immense wealth of the woman who was buying his gifts), he not only gave in but pointed with delight at any number of outfits, which Elise cheerfully bought.

Gloating over their purchases in the food court, Elise reopened the conversation. "So who do you think killed Jeff?"

Doan filled her in quickly on the possible suspects, not omitting Elise's adoptive mother from the list. "So you see, they all had motives."

"You forgot someone," she said.

"Oh?"

"Ronald Piebald."

"The guy from the Church of Dollars? We thought about him, but it seemed too farfetched."

"Not really. Especially since Jeff's current will leaves just about everything to the Church of Dollars. And I imagine if Jeff eloped with Tyler, he would change his will."

Doan choked on his gourmet Thai wrap. "Oh my god! I have to call Binky! I have to call Tim! I have to—"

Elise put a hand on his arm to calm him down. "It doesn't mean he did it. It just makes him another suspect."

"Yeah, but what a suspect! How much was Jeff worth?"

She shrugged. "Probably just short of a hundred million dollars."

"Are you kidding?!"

"No. I mean, look what he owned. Percentage points in *Total Carnage,* a part share in the Hollywood Cafe"—which Doan knew to be a series of chain restaurants that lured customers with the promise of appearances by the celebrity owners, none of whom ever visited any of the locations again after the opening night party—"the Jeff Breeze dolls, the Jeff Breeze fan club merchandise . . . it goes on and on. Piles and piles of money."

"That's enough money to kill for," he said. She looked at him. "Well, I don't mean *I'd* kill for it. Well, actually, it depends on who you asked me to kill. . . . oh, never mind."

"Is the Tim you have to call Tim O'Neill?"

"Well, yes."

"I'd like to meet him," she said.

"I'm sure he'd be delighted to meet you."

"Maybe we should all get together—you and your partner and Tim and Tyler and I—and brainstorm."

"That's a wonderful idea!" he said, delighted. Then he sobered. "You know this could get ugly. If we were to find out Jennifer did it, for instance—"

"I can live with that. Like I said, I didn't love Jeff, but I felt sorry for him. So I guess I want to be on the team that catches his killer. So when do I start?"

Doan smiled at her. "You just did."

NINE

Doan's hopes for a romantic working dinner with Tim were dashed that afternoon by a phone call from Binky.

"So how did it go today?" she asked.

"Oh, not too bad. I'm Elise Breeze's new best friend, I'm on the Breeze payroll, *and* I think I'm in love. And to think I have you to thank for all of it!"

"In love?! With whom?"

"The man you set me up with, dearie—Tim O'Neill."

"Oh yeah?" she asked; Doan could hear her eyebrow arching.

"Yes indeedy. Honey, he's tall, pale, has dark eyes, dark curly hair, he's smart, warm, fun, drives an Alfa Romeo. In fact, he's coming over for a working dinner tonight."

"Goody. Then I won't have you kvetching about me and Sam."

"Speaking of Sam, what are you doing tonight?"

"Why, nothing. That is, I'll be working tonight. With you and Tim O'Neill."

"*What?!*" Doan spluttered.

"Sure," she said casually. "We are a team, after all, aren't we?"

"I thought we were also friends," he said with a chill in his voice. "And friends don't let friends go without nookie."

"I just think you need a bit of payback for baiting me about Sam. And if it really is a *working* dinner, I should be there, don't you think?"

Doan sighed. "Fine. I guess *everybody* will be there. I might as well call Elise and have her come, too. Oh!" he shouted, remembering. "Guess what she told me!"

"Don't tell me on this phone," she said.

"Why not? Do you think Mary Duveen is listening in?"

"I wouldn't put it past her. I'll see you tonight."

Fortunately, Tim was the first to arrive for dinner, so Doan could at least count on a little light make-out session before the rest of the party showed up.

"Flowers!" Doan exclaimed with delight, accepting the spray of lilies. "I guess I did make an impression on you."

"I was afraid of what might happen if I *didn't* bring them," Tim said.

"You would have had to wait until the second date for sex," Doan explained, wrapping his arms around Tim and waiting—not long—to be kissed.

The door opened. "Oh!" Binky exclaimed. "I'm sorry. You must be Tim O'Neill."

"Tim, Binky," Doan sighed, unraveling himself from Tim.

Tim extended a hand. "Nice to meet you."

Doan had circled behind him and whispered theatrically in his ear, "You might not say that if you knew who she was dating."

"You are *so wrong* about Sam Braverman," Binky said defiantly.

"Sam Braverman? You're dating Sam Braverman?" Tim asked, astonished.

"Yes I am. I suppose you think he's the killer, too."

"Noooo, I just— Never mind."

"No, what?"

"Nothing. Really. I have nothing to say. No comment. End of conversation."

"Did you see the flowers?" Doan asked her, steering her into the kitchen. "Let it go," he whispered. "Sam Braverman is having Tim followed all over town since he started writing this article on Jeff Breeze."

"Ah," Binky said. "That would make for explainable prejudice."

"It certainly would! Now just remember to *be professional*. Sam Braverman may be your paramour, but he's also still a suspect."

"Okay, okay."

The doorbell rang. "I'll get it," Binky said. She opened it with a smile that faded in confusion. "Hello?" she asked the cherub at the door.

"Is Doan here?" Elise asked.

"Hi," Doan said, coming out of the kitchen, "Come on in. Tim, Binky, this is Elise Breeze. She'll be helping us out."

Tim was agog. He turned to Doan. "I thought you just worked fast on *me*."

Doan smiled serenely. "I always get my man."

"How's the article coming?" Elise asked Tim.

"Well, I, uh . . ." Tim was not the sort to be flustered; he'd grilled bigger celebrities than you or I will ever even glimpse, but Elise's startling blue-eyed directness had disarmed the tough reporter instantly.

"Don't worry," Doan said. "She knows everything, and she's on our side."

"Ah," Tim said.

"So what's your news?" Binky said.

Doan looked at Elise. "Shall I tell them?"

"Go ahead."

"Seems one of the suspects we dismissed shouldn't have been dismissed after all."

"Go on," Binky said impatiently.

"As it stood when he died, Jeff Breeze's will left everything to the Church of Dollars."

Tim's eyes widened as he made the connections. "Then . . . if he left his career and Jennifer and the Church of Dollars for your friend Tyler . . ."

"Exactly," Elise finished. "One hundred million dollars that does not go to Ronald Piebald and company."

The doorbell rang again. Doan looked at Binky. "You were expecting someone?"

Binky opened the door to find Sam Braverman. "Hi, I—" Sam stopped, looking around the room incredulously.

"Come on in," Binky said, pulling him into the apartment.

"Hello, Sam," Elise said.

"Hello, Elise." All present could tell he was dying to ask her what she was doing here. He got to do another double take on seeing Tim. "O'Neill," he said flatly, nodding.

"Braverman," Tim returned, mimicking him exactly.

"So!" Binky said brightly. "Sam! What brings you here?"

"Well, I just thought I'd surprise you."

"And I bet you never even gave him your address," Tim said, addressing Binky but looking all the while at Sam.

Sam smiled. "Still bitter after all this time, huh?"

"Still *relieved*, would be the word I would pick," Tim answered darkly.

"What is going on?" Binky demanded of Sam.

"Why don't you tell her?" Tim asked. "Oh, that's

right. I'm the one who spills secrets; you're the one who keeps them. Sam and I . . . dated. Briefly. Many years ago.''

Astonished silence filled the room. Binky turned to Sam. "You're—"

"Not gay," he said hastily. "Bi, basically. I would have told you eventually. It just didn't seem that important at this point in our relationship."

"Sam is used to withholding information until he absolutely has to impart it," Tim added.

"Would you please shut up?" Sam said with a scowl.

Doan took stock of the scene and realized quickly that an imminent fistfight was not out of the question. "Tim, dear, why don't you and Elise and I take a little walk?"

"Fine. But I wouldn't leave your notes around here if *he's* going to stay."

"That's it." Sam lunged at Tim, who ducked out of the way.

"Stop it!" Binky screamed. "Oh my god, this could not get any worse."

The doorbell rang. Everybody froze. "That's probably Mary Duveen!" Binky said. "She's the only one who's not here."

She opened the door. "Oh my god." And then again, "Oh my *god.*" For standing there was not only Kenny Wells, liberated from jail, but Kenny Wells accompanied by Luke Faraglione, San Francisco homicide detective and Binky's former paramour.

"Kenny!" Doan shouted with joy. "Luke!! Oh my god, what is going on?!"

"I'm free," Kenny said, sailing into the room and stopping at the sight of Sam. "No thanks to you."

"Free how?" Doan asked.

Luke took over. "Toxicology finally finished their report. Seems Jeff Breeze wasn't killed by the perfume, or not exactly, anyway. They found an agent in his bloodstream that is harmless—except when mixed with certain substances found in Closer. In other words, somebody poisoned Jeff *before* he got to Macy's.''

"And he was bound to get some into his system, with all those anorexics—no offense," Kenny said to Binky, who was currently incapable of noticing, let alone taking offense, "all those *merchandise assistants* spritzing everyone around him with the stuff. I was just the lucky stiff who gave him the big dose he needed to end his miserable life."

"So," Luke said to Binky, "aren't you going to introduce me to all your friends?" She let out a small groan and sat down on the floor.

Sam extended a hand. "Sam Braverman."

Luke's extended hand dropped to his side. "I see."

Binky looked daggers at Doan. "You've been *reporting* on me!"

"I just *mentioned* that you were seeing someone," he defended himself.

"Tim O'Neill," Tim said, extending his hand to Luke. "I'm not dating Binky."

"He's with me," Doan said, wanting Luke to feel that their side had the larger numbers. Luke introduced himself and shook Tim's hand.

"Well, now that we're all here, maybe we can do a little brainstorming." Everybody turned to Elise, and Doan introduced her to Luke and Kenny.

A short silence then fell. Tim glared at Sam. Luke glared at Sam. Binky glared at Doan. "You know," Elise continued, "Doan tells me that Luke here is the official investigator on this case. And the rest of us are way ahead of him as far as suspects go. Why don't we fill him in?"

"Doan has kept me up to date, thanks," Luke said, smiling at Elise.

"Not on the latest," Doan began, but Tim poked him in the ribs, indicating Sam. "Oh."

"Well," Sam said, "I guess I should be going." And he did just that.

Binky followed him out into the hall. "Wait!" she called, and he turned around. "I'm really sorry. I mean, I am really really sorry that you wanted to do something nice for me and ended up walking into a room with the two people in the world who hate you most."

Sam laughed. "There are people who hate me a lot more than my ex-boyfriend. Or yours. I'm the one who's sorry." He moved toward her, took her face in his hands. "The last thing I want is for you to think that I'm holding out on you. Or lying to you. I swear to you I did not kill Jeff Breeze, or have anything to do with having Jeff Breeze killed, or do I knowingly work for whoever killed him. Okay?"

Binky nodded, cupping her hands over his. "I believe you. Everyone seems to be saying I shouldn't, but I tend to trust my instincts. I'd better get back in there. I'll call you later."

Inside, Doan studiedly did not look at her. "Don't worry," she said, "I didn't tell him anything."

"I didn't think you did," Doan replied, eyes wide in mock injury.

While Binky had been outside with Sam, Doan had filled Luke in on the connection with the Church of Dollars. When she came back, Luke had them all sit down as he took command of the situation. "Okay, here's what we've got. We've got Mary Duveen, who knows all about Jeff's secret life, and has other secret lives to keep secret. Sorry, Binky, but the same has to be said about Sam Braverman. We've got Jennifer Breeze, who didn't want the public humiliation of being left for a guy. And we've got . . . What's his name?"

"Piebald," Binky supplied. "Ronald Piebald."

He smiled at her for the first time. "Thanks. That takes care of motive. Now we need opportunity. Now, this agent in Breeze's blood appears to have been applied less than twenty-four hours before he was sprayed with Closer. The coroner says it could have been applied transdermally—just brushed on the skin, didn't need a shot or anything. We need to know who was with Jeff Breeze in the twenty-four hours before his death."

"Sam would know that," Binky said defiantly.

"Sam is a suspect," Luke said flatly, "regardless of whether he's dating you or not. We need to get that information from other sources."

"Elise and I can check his datebook," Doan offered. "We've got the run of the house."

"I can check Mary Duveen's records," Binky said grudgingly. "She might have had him lined up for something."

"If you can find out where he was," Tim offered, "I can have my sources find out who else was there."

Luke rubbed his hands together. "Okay. Now we're getting somewhere." The sense of excitement was palpable in the room; the discord of only a few minutes ago was banished. As they talked excitedly, Doan went to the kitchen to dig out the takeout menus and get some food delivered. Tim followed him.

"Are you mad at me?" he asked Doan.

"For nearly provoking a fistfight with a man you obviously despise? No, actually, I thought it was quite exciting." He reached up and put his arms around Tim's neck. "Like a knight in shining armor going after a dragon."

Tim smiled. "A dragon I used to date."

"Well, he *is* gorgeous." Noting the look Tim gave him, Doan amended, "In his own way. Not as gorgeous as you, you being his moral superior and all." Their previously delayed make-out session postponed any further conversation on the subject.

Binky was left with Kenny, Luke, and Elise. "So," Elise said, knowing a situation that needed a conversation starter when she saw one, "Kenny, right? What brings you down here?"

Kenny smiled. "A little press conference I'm planning. I am going to blow the lid off *every closet door* in this town! And this time, I'm going to have *national media attention*! Prison, you see, has made me a very hot commodity."

Elise swallowed, plainly uncomfortable. "Um, can I talk to you for a minute, Kenny? In private?"

Kenny nodded suspiciously, but followed her into the bedroom. This left Luke and Binky in the living room.

"So I guess you've been pretty busy," he attempted. Then at a look from her, he hastily added, "I don't mean, you know, *that*. I mean, you've been working. And working undercover, too, I hear."

"Yeah, that's right. I think we're doing pretty well on our own."

"Uh-huh." He gave up. "Well, I should be going. I'm staying at the Ramada down on Santa Monica. Would you tell Doan he can reach me there?"

"I'll do that." She got up and walked him to the door. Watching him walk away, she called out faintly, "Luke."

He turned around instantly.

"I'm sorry. I mean, this was not the way I wanted to run into you again, you know?"

He smiled. "I know." And left.

Kenny and Elise emerged from the bedroom, Kenny a little less cocksure than he'd been before. He interrupted Doan and Tim in the kitchen. "Doan?"

"Yes, dear?"

"Um . . . Elise has set up a meeting; I guess she never had the opportunity to tell you about it, what with . . . all the people coming in and out of here. And she's asked me to go with her and you and Binky."

"Sure," Doan said. "A meeting with who?"

Kenny laughed. "With the most celebrated closet lesbian in this whole town. Tomorrow, the four of us are going to have tea with Charlotte Kane."

TEN

❧

The Breeze Town Car drove up to the apartment building the next morning, with Charlie at the wheel and Kenny and Elise in the back, the car having already picked Kenny up at the Ramada. "Aren't you supposed to be at work?" Kenny asked Binky once she and Doan were ensconced in the back.

"Charlotte Kane called Mary and asked to borrow her secretary. She concocted some story about hers being sick and the work being too confidential for a temp, blah blah blah."

"So," Kenny asked Elise, "how do you know Charlotte Kane?"

"We're both in AA."

"Is that Celebrity AA? Is there an AA that's just for celebrities?"

"Yes, there is. It's for famous people who don't want their image soiled by the public's finding out they're drunks and druggies. It's top secret, and you have to have had your picture in *People* at least twice to be admitted."

Kenny turned to Binky and Doan. "Is she pulling my leg?"

"Damned if I know," Binky said. "A couple days in this town and I'm starting to think anything's possible."

This time the car took them not to the Hollywood Hills but out to Malibu. The geography was different but the principle was the same—anonymous, gated entrances where you had to know your destination to find it. Doan had hoped for a chance for some stereotypical sunny beach frolicking, but the fog was thick and the coast was locked into almost San Franciscan grayness.

Charlotte Kane herself answered the gate intercom, and was waiting at her front door when the car pulled up. It was Doan's second close-up look at a movie star in as many days, and while Charlotte didn't have the elusive "it," it seemed to be so because she had willed "it" away from her. She was simply too smart to fall for "it"; that was written all over her face.

"Hello," she said, "come in."

Even Kenny was a bit awed by her. He'd written for years about movie stars as if they were so much commercial product, to be treated lightly, but he was not immune to star power in person. She led them to the living room, which had a breathtaking view of the ocean, where Binky discovered to her enormous surprise that "tea at Charlotte Kane's house" was to be taken literally; there were even scones. After everyone had cups in their hands, Charlotte spoke.

"I'd like to thank you all for coming here," she said, and for a wild moment Doan thought she was about to say "I'd like to thank the Academy." But then, that was because he was having a hard time taking his eyes off the two Oscars on the mantelpiece, one for acting and one for directing. "Especially you, Mr. Wells."

As Kenny fumbled for the appropriate thing to say, Binky realized that tea was not an affectation, it was a strategy. Charlotte wanted things to be civilized, and it's hard to hurl invective with a Limoges teacup in your hand.

"I know you haven't been treated well by the Hollywood community, especially during your recent incarceration." This was true; more than a few of those whom Kenny had targeted for exposure and abuse in his column had publicly crowed with joy at his incarceration. "So I appreciate your coming today to hear me out.

"I know that from outside the industry, things must seem a certain way. You see performers who are gay, or lesbian," she said, the comma evident in her diction and clearly intended to make a subtle statement about her own sexuality, "and you think, these people are sellouts. They're denying the truth about a part of themselves in order to cash in, and in the process, they're making it harder for other gay people in this country, because the country looks at the dream machine and sees only heterosexual faces, even on homosexual bodies. But I want you to look at this in a historical perspective. Think of the female writers of the nineteenth century who had to publish their work under a man's name—did they do that because they were embarrassed about being women, or ashamed of it? Or because the powers that be wouldn't take a woman seriously as a writer, if she wrote about something other than 'female subjects'? Do you ever wonder what it would be like to be an artist who couldn't create because of discrimination against his or her gender, or orientation?"

Kenny had found his voice. "There are a lot of gays, and lesbians," he replied, mocking her comma, "who act; the difference between you and them is that they don't hide who they are, and so they don't work in movies, and so they don't make as much money as you do."

"And whose fault is that," Charlotte pressed. "Is it my fault? Am I the one who decides that a gay person can't play a straight one? Or is somebody else making the decisions? What I'm saying is, you're blaming the collaborator, but not the dictatorship they collaborate with.''

"Meaning?'' Kenny asked.

"Meaning, if you want to go after somebody, I mean really go after somebody not because it will titillate your audience to find out that some favorite performer is gay, but to *change things,* then you need to raise your sights a little higher on the food chain. Studio executives, some of whom are even gay themselves, make these decisions. Why don't you beat up on them for not making more movies about gay people, for not hiring openly gay actors, for encouraging gay actors to stay in the closet?''

"Because they're invisible,'' Kenny said. "Because their fortunes aren't like yours—yours is based on how much the public loves you and is willing to pay to see you in a movie. Nobody has to love them for them to be successful. All they have to do is keep making the movies all of America wants to see, and they'll be rich and powerful forever.''

Charlotte smiled. "Unless you change that.''

"And how do I do that?''

"You can change your focus. You can stop obsessing in your column on Charlotte Kane and Ted Trask and Jeff Breeze, and start talking about Sam Braverman, and Mary Duveen . . . and about some gay executives whose names I'll give you.''

Kenny narrowed his eyes. "And what makes you think people will want to read about some nerd with green-lighting power rather than about your private life?''

"Look at the magazines today. I don't mean the celebrity-driven ones like *Pendennis* or *People,* but *Premiere,* or *Movieline,* or *Confidential.* People want to know the real inside scoop, the *real* scoop, not the PR Mary Duveen dishes out. So you've got your audience as mad as hell about closeted gay celebrities.

Fine! Great! Now what? Now you've got to explain the machinery to them. Now you've got to tell them about the agents and publicists who gang up and tell their clients not to come out of the closet, the casting directors who freeze out anybody who *is* out, the studio heads who limit gay characters in movies to second banana roles—"

"The gay friend," Doan added, "who always gets killed in the second reel. *Copycat! Single White Female!* The list goes on and on," he said helpfully.

"I want to help you," Charlotte said, overmastering Kenny with her clear green eyes. "You've outed me, again and again. Fine. Now what? Are you going to just keep on doing that? Or are you going to go to work on the systemic problem?"

Kenny was silent. Charlotte took an envelope off the tea tray and handed it to Kenny. "This is a party that's happening this weekend. If you're looking for the secret society of Hollywood homosexuals, this is it. If you want to out actors, you can take a pen and paper and write down everyone in attendance and fill your column for a year. But if you want to do something about the system, you can go and you can confront the men—the *gay men*—who make the decisions."

"I could make a scene," Kenny said with a smile. "I'm good at that, but what good would it do?"

"No. You should tell them who you are. Every one of them knows your name. And when they're done turning gray, you can talk to them. You can tell them you were going to throw a press conference and out half the people at the party, but that you're not interested in that anymore, you're interested in changing the system."

"Work within the system," Kenny said dubiously. "And why don't you do this, if it's such a good idea?"

Charlotte smiled. "For the same reason I don't come out of the closet. Because I'm scared. Because if you fail, nothing bad happens to you. But if I try . . . I love making movies. I love it so much. And it costs so much. It takes their money, their marketing machine, their distribution system, to do it. I'm asking you to do it for me, with my discreet help.''

Kenny looked to Binky and Doan. "What do you think?''

"I don't think thorny moral dilemmas are a strong suit for either of us,'' Binky said, and Doan nodded emphatically. "But I think she has a point. I mean, they can keep making closeted actors famous, and you can keep outing them, and they can keep replacing them, for ever and ever, can't they? Eventually, you have to do something about the machine that makes them, don't you?''

Charlotte Kane smiled. "More tea?''

"I don't know,'' Kenny said in the car. "I mean, there's a lot in it for her if I do it her way, do you know what I mean?''

Charlie the driver spoke up, surprising them all. "Charlotte Kane is one of the few people in this town I would trust. She's a real star, and a real lady.''

"What makes you so sure?'' Kenny asked snidely.

Charlie locked eyes with him in the rearview mirror. "I know her driver. He didn't get any health insurance working for her, but when his wife came down with leukemia, Ms. Kane paid all the bills.''

"Well,'' Doan said, impressed.

"Honestly,'' Elise began, "think of all the closeted gay stars in Hollywood. And think how many of them are pond scum, not because they're in the closet, but just because they're . . . assholes! If you could leave just one person alone, couldn't it be Charlotte?''

Kenny scowled. "Well . . . I don't know. 'Work within the system,' that's just shorthand for getting co-opted by the system.''

"Not if you really get the chance to knock over the big pins," Elise pressed.

"How old are you?" Kenny asked her.

Elise laughed. "Older than you know."

Kenny sighed. "All right. We'll do it Charlotte Kane's way—for a while," he finished darkly.

The following days found Binky spending more time than she had hoped actually working for Mary Duveen, especially while Doan in the meantime was spending his days cruising Rodeo Drive with Elise and "investigating" with Tim—she thought she had a pretty good idea what the two of them were investigating! Big ad campaigns were being prepped for several new movies, and it was Binky's duty to call a list of "critics" and get their fulsome praises.

"What's the story line?" Susan Craig asked Binky. Craig's name was unfamiliar to the majority of Americans, even though it appeared in ads for every movie that was issued by a major studio, since her invariably rave quote was invariably printed in thirty-point boldface caps, while her own name and affiliation—*American Movie Minute*, a show that existed solely as a Delaware corporation—appeared beneath in two-point type. Craig was not a real reviewer, but played one on TV, so to speak.

"It's Tom Cruise's latest film. You know, the usual Cruise formula: cocksure upstart gets his comeuppance, learns important lessons about life and love."

"Costarring?"

"Nobody important."

"Right," Craig said in her gravelly voice. "Hold on. Here: 'Tom Cruise is a knockout. A surefire Oscar contender.' Exciting conclusion takes place in . . . ?" she asked.

"Courtroom," Binky said.

"Again? Okay, uh . . . 'Don't give away the secret ending.' How's that."

"Fine," Binky said. She had already collected six of these, none of which were from people who had seen the movie, which was still being edited. Craig and her cohorts were paid top dollar to provide "advance buzz" for prerelease advertisements, buzz that only the most gullible filmgoer would fall for as no real reviewer printed a review until the film's actual release date had arrived.

Her other job consisted of sorting requests for interviews with Ted Trask, who also had a new movie coming up. Interviewers were grouped into several categories, the most exclusive being those who would actually sit down one-on-one with Trask. This was limited to a handful of movie magazines (*Confidential* excluded now, of course), the *New York Times*, the *L.A. Times*, and of course Cory Kissell of *Pendennis*. Then there were the pool interviews; these would involve the star sitting before a roomful of reporters who would all ask questions and then go home and write their articles in such as way as to look as if they, too, had gotten exclusive interviews. Then there were the tailored quotes, written by Mary's staff, for the Ted Trask fan club newsletters and miscellaneous other exceptions, such as Trask's hometown paper (the good opinion of the folks back home was irrelevant; that paper was included because it would have been bad PR for Trask to ignore them). And then there was everybody else, who would get press releases and stills from the movie suitable for reproduction in their august pages. This was a relatively easy process, but there were just so damn many people who wanted to talk to this jerk that Binky had her hands full keeping track of the piles of who got what.

Then Mary came out of her office. "I have an assignment for you."

Binky did her best, and thus did not scream. "Yes?"

"Ronald Piebald has been calling me, demanding a meeting. And frankly, he's just not important enough anymore." Now that the Church of Dollars's number one acolyte and Mary's number one client was dead, Binky thought. "So I'm sending you out to deal with him. I inflated your status, made it sound like you were in on my decisions, et cetera, you know, so that he didn't think he was getting a flunkie." Binky bit back her indignation. "Just tell him I'm very busy with Ted's new movie and the Oscars coming up so soon and I'm prostrate with grief over Jeff, blah blah blah, whatever it takes to get him off my back. Hell, I'd change my number to get rid of him if I wouldn't have to explain why I was changing it to so many *really* important people."

How the mighty have fallen, Binky reflected on the drive out to the Church of Dollars. One minute, heir to a hundred million bucks with the ear of the most powerful woman in Hollywood, the next . . . *pffft*.

The offices of the Church of Dollars were staffed with naught but beautiful women—probably all dolled up to look like heroines from an Evgenia Dollars novel, but it gave Binky more the feeling of being trapped in a Robert Palmer video. Piebald's own office, into which she was ushered without delay, was as splendidly tacky as she'd anticipated. Everything was gilded—the carpet was gold, with dollar signs woven into it, the heavy curtains were green with gold fringe, the desk was authentic Louis XIV and the mighty chair behind it was gold-plated with gold upholstery. The visitors' chairs were a mere American-dollar green. Hanging menacingly above Piebald's chair was a panoramic portrait of dour old Evgenia herself, a piece of socialist realism in which she led the bankers, lawyers, and other moneyed professionals over the barricades and into the heart of the cowering bureaucrats and welfare chiselers on the other side, waving a golden banner as she overcame the wretched masses.

"So now Mary is too busy to see me herself," Ronald Piebald said. The man belied his surroundings; he was anything but imperious and majestic. He looked like he might have been one of the unfortunate collectivists quivering in fear of Evgenia's might in the portrait above his head. He was possessed first off with the one personal characteristic Binky felt should be a capital offense: a comb-over, and a very pathetic one, as he was completely and undeniably bald on top. His suit might have been expensive-looking, before he ever put it on; now it was just a rumpled old sack. He wore the sort of hideous silver-rimmed spectacles that Medicaid gleefully inflicted on poor people. His dollar sign tie clasp was about to fall off.

"Mary is just overwhelmed. But as I'm sure she told you on the phone, I'm privy to everything Mary does."

Piebald lifted a dandruff-crusted eyebrow. "Oh? Then I can speak freely to you about 'the arrangement.' "

Binky didn't bat an eye. "We assumed that 'the arrangement' was why you wanted to speak to Mary."

"Are the documents safe? Is everything still in order?"

"To the best of our knowledge."

Piebald turned purple. "What do you mean, 'to the best of your knowledge'? Does she have the will or doesn't she?"

"She hasn't told you?"

Piebald narrowed his eyes at her. "Don't play games with me."

Binky might have been nervous playing fast and loose with Sam, but this little man wasn't worth half a Xanax. She decided to gamble that she did, after all, know something about the arrangement. "We have the last will and testament of Jeff Breeze."

"Yes, but do you have the *very last* last will and testament?"

She gave a little sigh of relief. So Mary knew about the plan to leave all Jeff's money to the Church of Dollars! "Unless we tear apart Tyler Anderson's apartment and Jeff Breeze's house, we can't know that for sure."

"Maybe we should call our friend and have him do just that, to make sure," Piebald said darkly.

Binky scrambled to recover. "And even if we did that, Jeff may have had a safe deposit box we know nothing about. We would just be alerting people that we weren't sure we had the final will."

Piebald nodded abstractedly. "Yes, yes. That's true. We just need to be absolutely sure that nobody produces a new will to annul ours. Can't . . . something . . . be done with Tyler Anderson?"

"What do you mean," Binky asked, turning cold.

"If anybody would know about a new will, wouldn't it be he? Wouldn't Jeff have told him? Our friend could get it out of him. He's done it before."

Binky felt nauseous at the idea of Sam beating people up. "I don't think we want to resort to violence if we don't have to. That might complicate things unnecessarily."

"Fine." He stood up. "You tell Mary that I want her to *make sure*—do you read me?—*make sure* there is no other will."

Binky stood as well. "I'll pass that on."

She did not shake in the lobby. She did not shake on the street. She shook in Mary Duveen's limo as she tried to light a cigarette. Of course it should have hit her before this that there was violence involved—after all, the whole point was that Jeff Breeze had been *murdered!* What this really meant was only now becoming clear to her. *Other* people could get murdered, too—Tyler, or even herself, now that she knew the secret. It was now more crucial than ever that Piebald never, ever talk to Mary Duveen again. But he could call her anytime! she thought in a panic, fishing in her purse for the half a Xanax she had only just dismissed any need for. If he could only get a word in edgewise before Mary hung up on him—Maybe it was time to quit working for Mary.

Maybe it was time to leave town.

"I don't get it," Doan said that night. "If she's in that thick with him, why isn't she taking his calls?"

"And why would she send you to deal with him? Why would she risk your finding out about the will?" Tim added.

"I don't know," she moaned. "Maybe she just thought he couldn't possibly be stupid enough to mention it to an underling. Maybe she thought he was just going to nag her about something else."

"But she told him you were her right arm," Elise added.

"Yeah, but he was supposed to know that was bullshit!" Binky said. "Everybody in this town makes their assistant sound important, so that people don't feel shit on when they get the assistant! She must have thought he's a lot smarter than he turned out to be."

Tim shook his head. "I don't think you should go back to work there. She's bound to call him after that and berate him for talking to an underling."

"And if I don't go back, then what? Then she'll *know* something is up. No. I'll go back. I'll just tell her that he started talking about the will and I played along, because I was supposed to know what she knew, right? I need to prove I'm her *loyal assistant,* right?"

Tim sighed. "I don't know."

Binky was irritated. "I don't know that it's your decision."

Tim threw his hands up in self-defense. "I'm sorry. You're right. But this means you're working for someone who now looks like she may very well have had a hand in Jeff's murder.''

"But," Doan asked, "what does she stand to gain from a will that leaves all the money to the Church of Dollars?''

"That," Binky said firmly, "is what I need to go back to find out.''

Later that evening, when the crowd had dispersed, Doan and Binky moved from martinis to black coffee.

"Honey," Doan said, "I really don't want you doing anything that's going to get you killed. I mean, if you were to die, what on earth would I do for amusement?''

"Most unselfish of you.''

"Oh, you know what I mean. Here. Let me put it this way: *I would much rather wear a pair of pants, to a job, five days a week, than see anything bad happen to you.*''

"Wow," Binky said, genuinely touched. "That means a lot to me, Doan. But let me put it to you this way: Since becoming a detective, I've felt like . . . like I'm doing something I like for the first time in my life. And it doesn't hurt that we're doing good in the process. I would rather run the risk of getting hurt—even *killed*— than go back to San Francisco with my tail between my legs and have to get *another dreary job that makes life completely unbearable.* How's that?''

"Well," Doan said. "The logic of that is impeccable, I have to say. I guess I feel guilty because you're in danger and I'm not. Not really.''

Binky smiled. "Well, hon, this case is still young. We'll see what we can do about *that.*''

The next day, Binky went into the lion's den. There was no time for her to compose herself; Mary was already there. "So what did Piebald want?" Mary asked.

Binky had thought long and hard about what to say

at this point. To lie would have been to rely on a providence so munificent it would ensure that Piebald never, ever got the chance to speak to Mary again, and right now Binky was feeling of little faith. No, the best thing would be to tell the truth, but to tell it as if she had no idea what that truth implied.

"He wanted to talk about Jeff Breeze's will. He wanted to know if you were sure you had the very last version of the will."

For the first time ever, Binky saw Mary lose her composure. The mouth of the most powerful woman in Hollywood dropped open, her eyes, already magnified to the size of silver dollars by her glasses, now took on the appearance of saucers. "And what did you say?" Mary asked calmly.

"I said as far as we knew, we did. I mean, you told him I was your right hand, so I had to pretend I knew what he was talking about. But that didn't really satisfy him; he wanted me to make sure you were sure there weren't any other later-dated wills floating around." Now she was ready to play dumb. "But wouldn't Jeff Breeze's attorney have his will?"

This succeeded in putting Mary on the defensive. "Of course he does. Ronald Piebald is just concerned because—Well, it'll be common knowledge when the will is read, so I'll tell you. Jeff left everything to the Church of Dollars."

"Everything?" Binky gasped theatrically. "What about the wife and kids?"

"Oh, she already has her own millions, from the— From the movies she made," Mary said. From the fee for the *arranged marriage*, you mean! Binky thought. "And I'm sure she'll provide for the children. The church meant a lot to Jeff, you see."

"I guess so!"

"Now, I knew that because I was Jeff's publicist and of course when this comes out in the press, people will be calling me to ask why he did it, so of course I had to know. Honestly, though," she said, returning to fine form as the ever-spinning Mary Duveen, "that Piebald is so greedy, he's so afraid there might be a will that even I didn't know about!"

"As if *that* would be possible," Binky said with a smile.

"That's right," Mary said assertively, as much to herself as to Binky. "Nothing like that could ever happen without my knowing all about it. Well!" she said, getting up in a manner that implied Binky's dismissal from her presence, "you did very well. Of course I don't have to remind you that something like this is to be kept in strictest confidence. I mean, it's one thing to leak little details about bad blood on the set to *Confidential*; I've had plenty of leaks here in my time! But this," she said, fixing her laser gaze on Binky, "is the kind of thing that *must not* be talked about outside this office. *Capisch*?"

"Got it."

"Good. You'll find a little extra something in your next paycheck for handling this so well. Spend it wisely!"

As was her wont, Binky did spend it, and not wisely, and before she'd actually gotten it—that night, in fact. She took Sam Braverman out to dinner, for once, instead of the other way around. It was an awkward evening at first, since most of what had gone on in her life since the last time she'd seen him was compartmentalized information. All the same, she still didn't think Sam was the bad guy in all this—well, at least not the baddest. It may have been shallow of her, but a man who could make love like that deserved *some* chance to prove himself.

"Can I ask you a question?" she asked.

"Shoot."

"Do you, or did you ever, work for the Church of Dollars?"

Sam smiled wryly. "Am I now or have I ever been . . . ?"

"I'm sorry it sounds like an inquisition. But I've promised . . . some people that I'll be careful what I tell you."

"I know you have. And considering my reputation—especially in the circles you're traveling in now—I can't say I blame you. But no, I've never worked for the Church of Dollars. I do have *some* morals, you know."

"And the C of D is immoral?"

"Don't you think so? A philosophy of 'every man for himself, no matter the circumstances'?"

"Very charitable of you. Not at all in concert with your image as a man who's willing to step on a few toes to get his clients what they want."

"I step on toes that aren't helpless. I step on paparazzi, on sleazy detectives, on tabloid reporters, on women who say my clients made them pregnant when they've never been in the same country."

Piebald's suggestion still rang in her ears. "Have you ever beaten anybody up? Or had somebody beaten up?"

"Not here."

"But you have beaten people up."

Sam let out a whoosh of air and leaned back in his chair, rubbing his brow. "When I was in the Mossad, we questioned a lot of terrorists. Terrorists who knew the plans and whereabouts of other terrorists. Sometimes we beat them up to get what we needed out of them. But that was in matters of life and death. Nothing in this town is really ever about life and death. Nothing here is worth doing that for."

"Thank you," Binky said. "That tells me what I needed to know."

Sam looked up at her. "You believe me?"

"I do. I believe you've threatened, and you've coerced, and you've blackmailed, but if you say you've never physically harmed anybody in your current profession, I believe you.''

"And what makes you think the Church of Dollars was going to have me beat somebody up?'' Sam asked.

"I didn't say that!'' Binky protested.

"But you did,'' Sam insisted with a smile. "You made a big mistake for a detective, Binky, you gave me a lot more information than you asked for. What's the C of D got to do with all this?''

"I don't know,'' she lied, not well, and she knew she hadn't lied well from the look in Sam's eyes. "Honestly!''

"Sounds like honesty is a one-way street tonight.''

"Oh, Sam, I'm just dying to tell you everything, but I can't! I have partners in this, you know? And none of them trusts you any farther than they can throw you.''

"Okay, then tell me this. Are you, yourself, in any danger?''

"Not yet. Not that I know of. Not unless Mary Duveen finds out I'm a phony.''

"Oh, she never will.''

"What makes you so sure?''

"The day she hired you, she called me and asked me to investigate you. I asked her to tell me what you'd told her, and I confirmed to her that you'd been working for Eleanor Van Owens for years as a personal assistant.''

"You knew! That day you called the office, you already knew I worked for Mary! You already knew you'd get me when you called! Wipe that smile off your face!''

Sam laughed out loud. "Of course I knew. There's not a lot I don't know.'' We'll just see about *that*, Binky thought. Suddenly she wondered if Mary *had* used Sam to make sure there were no other wills. Sam may have never worked for the Church of Dollars, but he'd done plenty of work for Mary. Could she ask him? She didn't dare. She didn't want to know the answer.

"I'm sorry," he said. "Come on, I'll make it up to you."

"How?"

"You'll see. Come on!"

It is not possible for us mere mortals to actually touch the HOLLYWOOD sign; the area around it is fenced off and the gate to the service road is padlocked, partly to deter vandals and partly because too many unhappy and theatrical-minded starlets had chosen to take dramatic leaps from the top of the *H*. Needless to say, Sam Braverman had a key to the padlock, and Binky soon found herself sitting in the dirt, reclining against one of the spotlights in front of the huge metal letters.

"Some view, huh?" Sam asked rhetorically. It was indeed some view. The whole enchilada was theirs to regard, the whole arena of contest, the whole—well, sorry! Make up your own clichés for the sight.

"Thanks," Binky said, moving closer to Sam both out of affection and out of the need for warmth—it was a chilly evening.

"So what happens when this case is over?" Sam asked.

"Well . . . I guess we go back to San Francisco."

"For sure?"

"Well . . . no," she said. Then, eager not to have him think she would chuck everything to stay with him, she added, "I mean, Doan may not go back. He really seems to have found Mr. Right this time, and Tim's job would keep him here."

"I guess even Tim O'Neill has to be somebody's Mr. Right," Sam said grudgingly.

"Some people would say the same thing about you," she reproved him.

He laughed. "Touché. And would you go back if he stayed?"

"I don't know." She wondered about that for the first

time. Doan wasn't just her partner in the detective business, he was her partner in crime! Who else could be so easily convinced to dine out lavishly, to spend with utter profligacy, to travel heedless of economy? It hit her for the first time that there really wasn't much else to tie her to San Francisco.

"I guess I'll cross that bridge when I come to it," she said noncommittally. "And what would I do down here? Be a secretary again?"

"In Hollywood, today's personal assistant is tomorrow's powerful producer."

"Hey—I've seen *Swimming with Sharks,* okay? I'm just not constitutionally suited to take that kind of abuse."

"Well, you could come to work for me."

She sat up. "What?!"

"Sure. You're a great detective. I could use you on my staff."

"Well, no offense, but, well, from what I hear," she emphasized, "some of what you do is just a little too ... what's the word I want? I don't mean sleazy, or criminal. Grimy! That's it."

"Hey, come on! What you do and what I do aren't so different. I mean, you're spying on Mary Duveen, aren't you? Working for her under false pretenses? Doan is the new Breeze nanny, and that's under false pretenses, too, isn't it? That's kind of grimy, isn't it?"

"No! I mean, we're doing it to solve a murder investigation."

"And when I do it ... ?"

Binky didn't hesitate. "You're helping rich and powerful people maintain a public image they don't deserve."

"Ow," Sam said, still smiling. "I guess that means no?"

"Well ..." Binky hesitated, reluctant to burn her bridges. After all, what if Doan *did* stay in L.A.? What

was the point of going back to San Francisco, where the
only person waiting for her was the ex-boyfriend she no
longer wanted to see? She'd have to do *something* to
supplement her meager trust fund. "I won't say no, absolutely, forever, but I will say no right now. Is that
okay?"

"Sure. I know there's a lot up in the air. When it gets
settled where you're going to live, and, you know,
maybe when this case is settled you might trust me a
little more—"

"I trust you," she insisted.

"As much as you can, when everybody around you
disagrees."

"Well, yeah."

Sam got up and offered her his hand. "It's cold. Let
me take you home."

That same evening found Doan comfortably ensconced
in Tim's house. Now, while Doan, as a younger man,
had lived for years off the good graces of other, older,
wealthier men (back before he started wearing dresses),
it could not fairly be said of him that he was a gold
digger. Like the cat he resembled, when he found a
warm and comfy spot, he settled down into it without
too much analysis of exactly what the heat source was.
Men were happy to give, and Doan was pleased to receive. After he grew his hair out and began wearing
dresses, there were fewer men willing to take him on,
as he no longer conformed to the gay American ideal of
young, boyish prettiness. Yet, again like a cat, when
thrown out the door into the cruel world, Doan had
landed on his feet, living off a multitude of little jobs
like weekend DJ at a popular club, record store clerk,
Binky's personal housekeeper, and, of course, the never-
ending, always-expanding generosity of the issuers of
revolving credit. Doan was always on the lookout for a

good man, but this had more to do with a desire for sex and companionship than for money.

That having been said, it certainly did not hurt to discover that Tim had, while not millions, a comfortable income. *Confidential* paid its star writer well, and he'd written several movie star biographies that had not disappointed his public or his publishers. His house was a modest one, a pink stucco affair on a street of houses built in the thirties, back when there was still a reasonable amount of space between houses and a reasonable diversity in the appearance of different houses—especially in L.A., where space was not at a premium and where aesthetic diversity could reach almost egomaniacal proportions. The house was light and airy, with plenty of windows facing onto the palm-studded street. It reminded Doan of Mildred Pierce's house at the beginning of the Joan Crawford movie.

Doan had already decided that Tim was quite a catch, house or no house (though it should be admitted that the Alfa Romeo clinched the deal). Nonetheless, Doan had been rich and he'd been poor, and he knew rich was better. To live in a house! he thought. Few and far between were the friends Doan could count in San Francisco who owned houses, the market there having been sacked by invading millionaire huns in the eighties who had driven prices to absurd heights for even the most pathetic dumps. To own property now in the Bay Area without being filthy rich was to have to live in some nightmarish suburban development, with about three inches between your house and the next, and neighbors who would never, ever be the sort of people who would take Doan to heart. And while Binky was already speculating whether or not Doan would return to San Francisco, leaving Tim behind, such thoughts hadn't crossed Doan's mind. Like many of us who live on revolving credit, for Doan, tomorrow was another day. The prospect of inevitable parting had not raised its head yet over

Doan's horizon. He was with Tim now, and he was enjoying himself. Nonetheless, his satisfaction in sitting with his dream man in a charming house in a temperate climate was working its magic on his subconscious. Somewhere down there was the Doan who had taken charge on the innumerable occasions when he'd been called upon to do so, and this deeper Doan was thinking about what the future would hold, and making a plan.

This sunny afternoon found Doan curled up on the couch, nestled within Tim's strong arms. "You know," Doan said, "I think we should start investigating the Church of Dollars. Check out their finances, stuff like that."

Tim untangled himself from Doan, got up, and went into his office. He came back with a copy of *Confidential* in his hand. "Already done."

Doan flipped through the magazine until he found what Tim was talking about. " 'A Clear Conscience For Sale: Inside the Church of Dollars, by Tim O'Neill.' I should have known. Gosh, it's long! Can you give me the *Reader's Digest* condensed version?"

"Well, you know a lot of it already. Evgenia Dollars set it up, with Piebald in charge. It basically spent her money proselytizing her 'philosophy' until the seventies, when est and all those movements got so hot—and profitable. That was when Piebald transformed the C of D into a self-help movement, charging astronomical sums for 'seminars' on 'clearing your guilt circuits,' that kind of thing. It went into a slump in the early eighties, because people no longer needed Evgenia Dollars to tell them making money at all costs was a good thing."

"Then Ted Trask came along."

"Right. With a real Hollywood star as their spokesman, more like their pied piper, they lured suckers into the church who were willing to part with their money for a chance to meet Ted Trask, and later Jeff Breeze, as well as all kinds of B-list stars who signed up basically for the same reason anybody joins a cult—because they found the church would take them seriously. And, of course, if you were in the industry, being in the C of D was a way to get introduced to Mary Duveen, who could make you an A-list star.''

''Is she a member?''

Tim laughed. ''Hell, no! Mary Duveen doesn't need anybody to tell her that unbridled power is a virtue. But she found it was good press for Trask and Breeze to belong, even if it was sometimes negative press—all publicity being good publicity. She basically treated Piebald like any other power player in town, until Trask's career dived and Breeze died. Then he was just another agent without any important clients.''

''So the whole thing really mushroomed. Sounds like they're raking in the dough. Why is Jeff Breeze's money so important?''

''Well, first off, because there's so damn much of it. When I did that article a few years ago, I estimated the net worth of the C of D at about $25 million. The other thing is, Piebald goes through money like water. Corporate jets, Tahitian 'retreats,' that office Binky told us about. Even millions doesn't last that long at that rate of expenditure.''

''Just ask Fergie!'' Doan nodded.

''Plus there's a difference in this town between money and *serious money*. Being a millionaire here is easy. Being a multimillionaire isn't so hard. But a hundred million and up—*that's* what makes you a real player in this town. With that kind of money, Piebald could buy national airtime for commercials, send spokespeople around the country, even put up political candidates—anything he wanted, really.''

''And 'this town' being what it is, he'd be willing to kill to obtain the kind of power held by people he'd only fawned at the feet of all this time.''

"For a lot of people here, the only reason to eat shit every day is in the hope that someday, you can make somebody eat your shit."

"Charming," Doan said dryly. "I'm going to mix a pitcher."

"What are you going to wear to that party tomorrow night?"

"Party? Oh, right. The one Charlotte Kane gave us the invite to." The group had determined that Doan, Tim, and Kenny Wells, being the group's gay male contingent, would be the least suspicious partygoers. "What do you think?" Doan asked. "Would it be in the best interests of the investigation for me not to wear drag?"

"I think so. But I think we can come up with something you won't mind."

Doan returned with a pitcher of martinis and set it down. "Oh? I don't think you've got anything I can wear." He put his hands on Tim's broad shoulders. "You're so much bigger than I am."

"I thought we'd make a little trip down to the Armani boutique."

"I can't afford to! I nearly maxed out my new corporate card at the Beverly Hills Hotel—more on room service than on the room, just between you and me— and my personal cards . . . well, I don't want someone I might be seeing on a regular basis to know just how deep in debt I am!"

"Then let me buy you a little something," Tim pressed, wrapping his arms around Doan's waist.

"Oh, thank you, but I don't think so. I don't want to be indebted like that to you."

"You let Elise buy you three John Galliano outfits," Tim countered.

"How do you know that!" Doan said, miffed.

"I'm a reporter, it's my job to find things out. You *could* ask Elise to take you out shopping again, this time for men's clothes—"

"I never asked her in the first place," Doan said. "She *volunteered*."

"Fine. Now I'm volunteering. What's wrong with that?"

"You don't have as much money—as much *ill-gotten* money—as she does. She was willing to spend it because it wasn't hers."

Doan separated himself from Tim, poured them each a drink, handed one to Tim, looked him in the eye, and spoke. "Many times in my life I have accepted expensive gifts. My apartment, for instance. Mostly because the people who gave them to me were filthy rich, and wouldn't miss it. But I've never taken something like that from somebody . . . well, from somebody I'm emotionally interested in. It just creates . . . an imbalance. And that's fine, when someone is basically purchasing your services, be that as bed partner or just ornamental decoration, but—" Doan sighed. "I really like you. In fact, I'm mad about you. And you have a lot more money than I do. Hell, more than someone like me ever will! And I just don't want this relationship, if a relationship is what it turns out to be, to start off with you spending inordinate sums of money on me." He clinked his glass against Tim's. "Okay?"

"How about Emporio Armani?"

"No."

"Armani Exchange?"

"I can still afford *that* myself," Doan said indignantly. He softened. "However, if you'd like to drive me there in that fabulous car of yours, I wouldn't complain."

"At last," Tim said, kissing Doan softly on the lips, "your wish is my command."

ELEVEN

If anything was different for Binky at work now, it was that Mary Duveen was probably more trusting of her. The door tended to stay open now even when the likes of Jennifer Breeze called. Binky surmised that Mary couldn't really go very long in her line of work without an assistant becoming privy to plenty of confidential information—then again, this was quite possibly why she fired so many of them, so that no one of them could ever know as much as Mary herself did, and be able to work for, or even become, her competitor.

One morning Binky was sitting at her desk, munching a napoleon and thumbing through an advance copy of *Weekly Variety* when, much to her surprise, her cell phone rang. Mary had provided this phone to Binky as a sort of electronic leash, so that Binky would never miss a call from Mary, even if she were in the bathroom, say, or in the middle of sex with Sam, those being the two events that had so far been most likely to provoke the wretched thing into ringing.

"Yes, Mary?" she said into it, assuming Mary had gotten her numbers scrambled and called the cell number when she meant to call the office number—Mary was renowned in Hollywood for often calling the wrong number, getting a studio head when she meant to call one of her own clients, but she almost always found a reason to keep talking to the person she'd dialed by mistake, and the habit had become one of her "charms."

"It's me," Elise said. "You told us you thought Mary listened in on your office number, so I thought this would be safer. Is she there?" Even the unperturbable Elise was at least a little frightened of Mary, more out of caution than primal fear.

"No, she's arranged to have her hair done at the same time and place as Barbra Streisand, so she can talk her into something or another. What's so urgent?"

"I found out where Jeff went the night before he went to San Francisco."

"You found his datebook?"

"No, stupid me, I looked and looked for it until I finally thought to ask Charlie. He took Jeff to Ted Trask's house for dinner that night."

"Ted Trask? Who else was there?"

"I don't know. Maybe Mary knows. Can you look and see if she scheduled it?"

"She usually doesn't have anything to do with stuff at people's houses," Binky said doubtfully. "Everything she arranges is for public consumption. Charlie didn't see who else arrived?"

"No. I know Jennifer went, too."

"So then, it might have been Ted Trask who poisoned Jeff, but then again, it could have been Jennifer."

"Think about it," Elise said. "Ted Trask, avid member of the Church of Dollars, which stands to gain from Jeff's death, but maybe not for much longer if he changed his will in favor of Tyler."

"You're suggesting Ted Trask killed Jeff? That doesn't seem like that much of a motive."

"I'm suggesting nothing. But Jeff was at his house the night before he died."

"How could we possibly test your theory?"

"I've got a plan to do just that," Elise said mysteriously.

Later that afternoon, Binky found herself awaiting the arrival of Ted Trask at MDA. She couldn't concentrate on her reading, and sat looking out the window, nervously fingering a bottle of Closer, Jeff Breeze's signature cologne—which, incidentally, had already been discontinued by the manufacturer out of respect to the family due to the tragic events (and of course due to those events' impact on the marketing plan) and which as a consequence was already being hawked in the classifieds for three hundred dollars a bottle. Binky had winced in pain on discovering that the large tester bottle she had lost in the crowd that day was already worth five grand. Elise had messengered this bottle over to her as part of her plan.

Binky kept reminding herself that it was a perfect plan; if it went wrong, it would mean nothing. Her concern was, that it just might go right, and she would be alone, with the murderer, in a room on the top floor of the building, far away from anybody who could hear her cries for help. Then it was too late—the door opened, and there was Ted Trask.

In his youth, Ted had truly been a sight for sore eyes. His blond magnificence had reached its ripe zenith in the midseventies, and even then, when America's brief-lived zest for dark, ethnic types had also reached its peak, he was a star of the first order. Even those who didn't care for blonds had a thing for *him*. It had been the particular programming genius of Walter Weiss, a man still cranking out hits on TV today, to create a show that featured three beautiful female detectives *and* one beautiful male detective, who spent as much time on-screen as the girls did, waving a gun while wearing as little as possible. This was successful partly because Ted Trask had the face of an angel, the body of a god, and, crucially, the perfectly manageable hair of a real star. But what really made Trask a star was, frankly, his assets in the genital department, which were so obvious that no amount of concealment could hide it, and eventually the policy of doing so was abandoned. There was one episode of *Street Sirens* in the first season in which someone just plain "forgot" to tuck Trask (or so they said when anybody asked; certain groups opposed to sex on general principle had accused the network of doing it deliberately). When that episode was rerun, word of mouth made it the highest-rated piece of one-hour episodic television ever. After that, Trask went untucked for three successful seasons, his run on the show ending only when one of the Street Sirens overdosed on drugs at around the same time the prostitution arrest record of another was discovered, all unfortunately at the same time the country got into a moral dither and elected Reagan president.

Trask's career went into the usual tailspin: special guest appearances on *Fantasy Island*, a role as the deranged stalker in a made-for-TV "womjep" movie (as these staple "woman in jeopardy" flicks were known in the television industry), dinner theater in Florida, several stays at the Betty Ford Clinic, two divorces, a palimony suit (he won), and a paternity suit (he lost).

Then he'd discovered the Church of Dollars, or more to the point, the Church of Dollars had discovered him. The nineties, like the seventies, were good to Ted: After the excesses of the eighties, recovery (or at least the appearance of it) was the hot thing to do. Trask got off cocaine, lost the alcoholic bloat and nasty attitude that had driven away even the hardest-core of his few remaining fans, and found redemption on *Oprah*, penning one of the many staple Hollywood memoirs of the early nineties, all of which could basically be called "How Hollywood Fucked Me Up and Over." He was one of those people whose bodies were truly magnificent in more ways than one—despite years of booze and pills and lack of exercise and sometimes even fresh air and sunshine, after six months with a Church of Dollars–sponsored personal trainer and personal chef (and, a less well known fact, an excellent plastic surgeon), Ted Trask emerged from his dark chrysalis and graduated as only the most bathetic of Hollywood losers can into the town's exalted rank of those immortals known as "survivors." The very fact that he was still alive was amazing, his physical transformation into something resembling his younger self even more so. And where others gave the credit to NA or AA, when Ted Trask began hawking his (ghostwritten, of course) memoir on TV, he extolled the Church of Dollars and its philosophy of pure self-interest as his savior.

Certainly, it *had* been pure self-interest that had saved him, though not the kind he talked about; rather, it was Ronald Piebald's burning jealousy of the Church of Scientology's ability to round up stars like cattle that had inspired him to try and snag a star of his own, even if it meant spending countless of his precious holy dollars on the rehabilitation of a forgotten seventies TV star. Piebald even oversaw the jewel in the crown of the publicity blitz: Trask's marriage to a beautiful C of D member, handpicked by Piebald himself. The event was covered like Madonna's wedding to Sean Penn; Trask found himself with a career again and Piebald with a poster boy.

The only flaw in the plan was that rumors about Trask's sexuality had dogged him since the beginning, though such rumors Piebald quashed ingeniously. He would say that fat, ugly, straight men, refusing to accept that their women were more attracted to Trask than to themselves, consoled themselves by saying that "anybody that pretty must be queer.'' It was just what men in this country always said about better-looking rivals, until the fitness craze in the eighties started producing enough good-looking straight men that the ugly ones had to stop calling them all queer. In truth, Ted's sexuality was still a mystery, even to experts like Kenny Wells. Certainly there were several years in the eighties which Trask could not remember, and in which just about anything might have happened, and probably did.

And now, here he was, across the table from Binky. ''Hi, I'm Ted Trask,'' he said, extending a hand.

Binky had been too young to be indoctrinated into the teen cult of Ted at that time, although her sisters had papered their room with the posters of Trask which had sold by the millions back then. ''How do you do,'' she said, wondering only briefly as she looked into his cold blue eyes if he could have deliberately poisoned Jeff Breeze.

''So Mary wanted to see me right away?''

''Is that the message you got? That's not the message I left with your agency,'' she said, looking perturbed. ''I said Mary wanted to *talk to you* right away, but you didn't need to come down. Well, she'll be here momentarily. Can I offer you something?''

He sat down on the leather sofa. ''No, I'm fine, thanks. What's that behind your back?''

''Huh? Oh, that!'' She laughed nervously. ''It's sort of a black market item right now. A bottle of Closer. Have you smelled it?''

He jumped up. ''Uh, no.''

She approached him. ''Would you like to try it?'' This, she chose to think idly at this inopportune moment, was the reluctance she'd been expecting at Macy's that day, sure she'd have to insist people take a whiff.

''No! I mean, I'm allergic. Please keep that away from me.''

Binky had what she needed. She put the bottle down

on the desk. "Of course, I'm sorry. I should have thought of that. I guess a lot of people are allergic. Why, now they're even saying Jeff Breeze might have been allergic to it himself!" She winced; she hadn't meant to go so far! She had wanted Trask's fear to emerge, not his suspicion.

He looked at her for a moment, narrowing his eyes. "Is that so?"

"Well, yeah. I mean, that's what it says in the papers," she lied. Then again, maybe it wasn't a lie—after all, she hadn't read a non-trade paper in some time. She could only hope that Trask hadn't either. She looked at her watch. "I'm sorry, Mary should be here by now."

Trask moved toward the door. "Well, I don't feel like waiting. I'll call her in the car."

"Okay, sure." She smiled, as sweetly as Miss Porter's had taught her to do. "I'm really sorry you came all the way down here for nothing."

He smiled. "That's all right. Bye."

Once he was gone, Binky collapsed in her chair. He was terrified of the stuff! She rang Elise immediately.

"What happened?" Elise demanded.

"He ran away. He was petrified of getting spritzed. What was the point of this?"

"I didn't want you to know, then, you not being an actress and all." Binky wondered about this; she'd played several roles to the hilt lately, but she said nothing. "It means that if he applied something that night to Jeff, he came into contact with it himself. Maybe he put it in Jeff's food, maybe he put it in all the food, maybe he managed to wipe some on Jeff but got some on himself. At any rate, he sounds like he knew what happens when the stuff mixes with Closer."

"Has—has there been anything in the papers about how they think Jeff died? I mean, after they released Kenny, did they say anything?" Binky asked.

"I don't know. Why?"

"I, uh, might have slipped up. I said I read in the paper that Jeff might have been allergic to Closer."

"Don't worry about that," Elise said.

"Why not?"

"Do you have any idea how much media there is in the world? In this town? How much idle speculation? Why, I'd bet the farm some tabloid has probably said just what you said. The point is, there's *too much media* talking about Jeff's death; Ted could never figure out that you hadn't read that *somewhere.*"

Binky relaxed, a bit. "I wish you still drank."

"You could use a drinking buddy right now, is that it?"

"Yeah."

"I'll pick you up. I know a place you can get a good martini, and I can get a decent Shirley Temple."

Later, while Binky and Elise calmed their nerves with their beverages of choice, Tim and Doan were dressing for the party and, what was more difficult, dressing Kenny for the party. Not only had Kenny brought nothing suitable to wear, he didn't even *own* anything that would have been suitable, his daily uniform consisting as it did of ACT UP T-shirts, tattered jeans, work boots, and a leather jacket. Tim was too tall to be able to provide anything from his closet, and Doan had already had to make a special trip for an outfit of his own. Convincing Kenny to partake of Tim's largesse and let Tim buy him something for the occasion had been even harder than convincing Doan, for different reasons.

"I already feel like I'm being co-opted," Kenny protested. "It's bad enough we're doing this at all, meeting these people, shaking their hands. Now you want me to dress like them, too."

"Don't think of it like that," Tim cooed. "Think of it as going undercover."

"Look," Kenny said flatly. "If I show up looking like them, acting like them, playing their game, they're going to *relax*. They're going to know I'm not a threat to them anymore. They won't even bother to take me seriously!"

"You don't understand this town," Tim pressed. "If you show up in Armani, it'll throw them. They *expect* you to be in a leather jacket, looking like a mad bomber. If you look like them, it'll feel like criticism from one of their own, and they just may pay *more* attention to that."

Kenny scowled, but eventually gave in. Tim was in no mood to economize, and bought him a top-of-the-line Armani suit. "All this could have been yours," he whispered to Doan as they watched Kenny modeling the suit in the store.

"I have an Armani suit," Doan countered. "Several, in fact. They're just not *men's* suits. He does look good in it, doesn't he?"

He did at that. In fact, he looked even better in Armani than he'd looked under arrest. The sight reassured Doan that their intrepid gang would at least get in the door.

That night they wound their way up the Hollywood Hills, the three of them tucked awkwardly into Tim's Alfa. "Here's the place," Tim said.

The place in question was the estate of Alex Lebedev. *Estate* was the proper word, as the land mass of the property rivaled that of more than one European duchy. Lebedev was the richest and most powerful gay man in Hollywood; he had built an empire, transforming a single video store in the bad part of L.A. into an international film distribution network. When the Japanese had come to Hollywood during their misguided quest for purveyors of soft product to complement their dominance in the field of hardware, Lebedev was one of many who cashed in on the Japanese willingness to spend billions of dollars on companies that were worth nothing even close to what they paid for them. This transaction had transformed him from a very wealthy man into one of the superrich, as in, top-of-the-*Fortune*-list rich.

Lebedev had concealed his homosexuality for decades, although it was common knowledge in a town driven almost entirely on gossip. Yet, this was part of the game in Hollywood: Everybody may know you're gay, but you don't talk about it in public. And as long as you don't talk about it, it's still all right to do business with you. But finally, with the advent of his Japanese billions, Lebedev came out—eventually. Such was the nature of the inherent paranoia about homosexuality in the industry that even this massively rich man, with whom nobody would now dare to refuse to do business, faggot or no, went about his coming out hesitantly. Like any celebrity eager to do some image control, he agreed to an interview with *Pendennis,* in which, in the proud tradition of rock musicians, he announced his "bisexuality." This has been and remains a popular avenue in the rock and roll world—one can put a toe in the water, so to speak, and if the water is too hot, one can always marry a member of the opposite sex, saying, "I *told* you I was *bisexual!*" As always, *Pendennis* did as it was told and printed Lebedev's announcement without criticism, comment, or investigation. No mention was made in the article of the press conference held several months earlier by a gay porn star who outed the billionaire by declaring himself Lebedev's lover, at the same time announcing his impending palimony suit. (The porn star died of a drug overdose before the suit went to court; tongues wagged about Lebedev's involvement, but the boy was known to have lived a fast life anyway and had died without any help from his powerful enemy.) Several gay papers printed details of that press conference, but the straight media, as was its wont, "respected the privacy of the persons involved," as it only ever does when the subject is homosexuality. Tim had wanted to do a story for *Confidential,* but Lebedev leaned on the owner and the piece was killed; needless to say, Tim had no love for Lebedev. Some months after the *Pendennis* story, when Lebedev realized that people in Hollywood were laughing at the announcement of his "bisexuality," he did an interview with the *New York Times* and officially came out of the closet.

With billions to play with, Lebedev set out, as Mary Duveen had done on a much smaller scale, to build a monument to his own ego. He wanted two things, seemingly irreconcilable: a massive estate on a par with those of the old studio heads of the thirties and forties, and a view from the Hollywood Hills. Being a billionaire, and a man nobody in town could now say no to, he got both his wishes.

Lebedev took the concept of the "teardown" to new levels. The teardown was, until his advent, the supreme hallmark of Tinseltown vanity: One bought an extremely expensive house, sometimes only a few years old, tore it down, and built a new one in its place. The reason given was usually that the property was perfect, but the house wasn't, or some such excuse. The reality was that few rich and powerful people could bear to hear their residence referred to by the name of its previous, far more famous occupant, those doing the tearing down and replacing usually being bean counters knocking down houses once belonging to movie stars.

Lebedev didn't just tear down a house, though. He found a hilltop that was perfect for his estate, and he bought about a dozen properties. He then not only tore down all the houses but leveled the top of the hill to make sure there was plenty of room for swimming pools, tennis courts, elaborate gardens, and a grand vacant lawn in front of the magnificent mansion, a lawn the size of several demolished properties, whose vast expensive emptiness advertised the owner's brute economic power.

There was no need for an Armed Response sign outside the gates of the estate; armed guards patrolled the perimeter at all times, and one was posted outside to take our party's invitation and buzz them through the gate. The road to the house turned into a carriage circle, but as they got up to the house proper they saw that the circle dipped down at that point, leading into a vast underground parking garage, which Lebedev had had built in anticipation of the large parties that he was so fond of throwing.

"That's so L.A.," Doan murmured.

Tim handed his keys to the valet attendant, who whisked the car into the bowels of the earth. "You know, you're only allowed to say that once during your time here."

"And don't you think I've chosen the occasion well?"

"Yes," Tim admitted. "It *is* so L.A."

They took a breath and stepped through the open doors and into the house. If it all looked vaguely familiar, Tim had warned them, there was a reason for that: Many of the rooms were copies of sets from Lebedev's favorite movies, which explained the *Gone with the Wind* staircase at the foot of which they now stood. (With the penuriousness exclusive to the very rich, Lebedev had also chosen this scheme because it saved him money on his interior design bill.)

After depositing their coats in a coat check room courtesy of *The Thin Man*, they looked to Tim for guidance. Doan had certainly been to wonderful parties in his youth as a celebrated beauty, but never on such a scale

as this, and Kenny was completely out of his element.
"Well," Tim said, "shall we mingle?"

"Mingling" was easier said than done. They quickly
deciphered the dynamics of the party: They would enter
a set—er, room—where those present would check them
out; everyone would ask everyone else who you were,
and inevitably there was somebody who recognized the
ubiquitous Tim O'Neill. As soon as it was clear that the
new people were unimportant, merely press and press's
guests, backs were smartly turned.

"Come on," Tim said. "Let's go where the real action is."

Doan and Kenny quickly discovered that, like circles
of paradise—or of hell, for that matter—the party was
divided up into coteries of varying shades of importance.
The outer rooms where they had started were for assorted riffraff: production assistants, personal assistants,
personal trainers, the more attractive mailroom clerks
from various talent agencies (their looks being the guarantee in Hollywood that they would rise quickly out of
the mailroom, beauty never being allowed to sink below
the level of dignity necessarily accorded to it in the industry), and the like. These were people invited because
(*a*) they were physically attractive and (*b*) they might
very well be more important tomorrow than they were
today, and thus worthy of cultivation by Lebedev—not
yet worthy of a personal benediction, of course, but it
never hurt to dispense such small favors as an invitation
to a party featuring a cast of hundreds if not a thousand.

The next circle Tim guided them to was outside by
the pool.

"It's so dark out here," Doan complained. There was
the glow from the pool and, a little further out, from the
spotlit fountain in the gardens.

Tim explained. "Lebedev likes an atmosphere at these
night parties that makes it amenable to his guests' han-
kering for nookie. He's rumored to watch via hidden

cameras on closed-circuit TV in his bedroom. Though somebody told me he made it easier to get laid out here so that people would stop leaving stains on his furniture.''

Out here they found less attractive but more powerful men, wearing better clothes and most all of them talking not to each other but into their cellular phones.

"Who are they calling at this hour?" Kenny asked.

"Their personal assistants," Tim replied. "Some of whom are in the rooms we just went through, answering their own cell phones."

"And they're too good to go ask in person?"

"That's part of it. But also, God forbid someone allowed out here should go *down there,* where the peons are partying. You might not make it back out here!''

"What do you mean," Kenny asked, " 'allowed out here'? How do you figure out where you're allowed to go?"

"You just do. You walk into a new room, realize everybody else there is older and richer than you, and you turn around. You're just supposed to know where you belong; if you don't, you don't belong here at all."

"Well," Kenny said grimly. "Then let's go where the *real* power is."

They reentered the house and mounted the Tara-esque staircase. "Lebedev's personal guests will all be up here," Tim said. Sure enough, after a short amount of time spent wandering around, they found a hum of activity from behind a pair of closed doors, guarded by a suited thug.

"Ten to one he's from Sam Braverman's outfit," Doan whispered.

"I wouldn't bet against that," Tim said.

The guard stood up at their approach. "Can I help you gentlemen?"

Tim pulled out a piece of paper and handed it to the guard. It was on Charlotte Kane's personal Tiffany stationery, asking Lebedev ("Dear Alex") to extend every courtesy to her friends. The guard may have looked stupid, but he was not—Sam Braverman did not hire stupid people for door duty at a party like this. The note had the desired effect; the guard knew the economics of Hollywood; he would pass the note on to Lebedev, who would file it away as "one favor done for Charlotte Kane," to be cashed in at a later date when he had need of that major star for one of his own projects. And the doors were opened.

Kenny almost gasped. This was it, the mother lode, the Ultima Thule of closeted faggotry. He needed little help from Tim in this room. There, talking with a stunning boy (the most extraordinarily beautiful young men were promoted to this room to be used as party favors), was the star of that long-running sitcom featuring the wise and wisecracking mother and children and the bumbling, adorably incompetent father. And there, by the bar, was that stand-up comic who couldn't stop getting arrested in the Beverly Center toilet (and who always escaped the charges and the publicity, thanks to Sam Braverman), talking to the *Pendennis* photographer whose relationship with a reclusive, mystical matinee idol was the hottest affair in Hollywood since Cary Grant and Randolph Scott. And who was that? Why, it was that former child star who'd been high on Ecstacy ever since his fourteenth birthday! And could that really be the pop star who'd stayed in the closet with the press's full cooperation, despite his having been repeatedly outed by Boy George in Boy's many interviews on the subject of his musical peers?

Yes, they were all here. Charlotte Kane had been right, Kenny thought: There was enough material here tonight to fill his columns with an outed celebrity a week for the next year. "Do you have a pen and paper?" he asked Tim.

"Oh no you don't. We're here under sufferance of

Charlotte Kane, and we're going to do it her way."

"Oh, shit. I should have known *he* would be here,"
Kenny groaned.

"Who?" Doan asked.

"Where else would their lapdog play but at their
feet?" Tim replied.

"*Who are you talking about?*" Doan asked insis-
tently.

Kenny pointed to a short, balding man looking up
adoringly into the face of America's current favorite un-
derwear model. "There. Cory Kissass, in the flesh."

"Let's move," Tim said. He and Kenny swept across
the room; Doan did his best to follow. They flanked
Cory Kissell and each took an arm. "Cory, can we talk
to you outside?" Before Kissell could protest, Tim and
Kenny had him out the French doors onto the balcony.

"O'Neill, what the *fuck* are you doing here?" asked
an angry Kissell. "This isn't your kind of party, there
are no *drag queens* here, or naked go-go boys. And I
can't imagine Alex inviting you."

"Oh, he didn't. We're here on business."

Cory snorted. "What kind of business?"

"A *murder* investigation," Kenny said dramatically.

"Oh, I see. Jeff Breeze was about to come out, and
you figure one of these closet cases offed him to save
the secret society? Am I right?"

Tim didn't blink. "How did you know Jeff was coming out?"

Cory shook his head and looked out over the gardens.
"Do you really think there are any secrets in this
town?" When he got no response, he continued. "Jeff's
little boy toy must have told his best friend, who was
probably supposed to keep it secret but, being a fag,
could never do *that* with such a juicy piece of gossip."

"Do you think you-know-who and you-know-who
and you-know-who knew?" Doan asked, prompting a
look of irritation from Tim. "Sorry."

"You mean did Jennifer Breeze know?" Kissell asked. Doan had actually meant Mary, Sam, and Ronald Piebald, but he let this slide. "Nah. The wife is always the last to know, right? Ha ha ha!" He slugged back the remains of his drink. "I gotta go."

But his attempt to go back inside was thwarted by Kenny. "Not so fast, *asshole*. If Jeff Breeze is dead because somebody needed to keep the secret that he was gay, then *you're* the one who killed him. *You're* the collaborator in this group," he continued, stabbing Kissell in the chest with a finger with each "you." "*You're* the one who helps keep it a dirty, shameful secret by putting whatever these closet cases say into your articles without ever contradicting them, no matter if you know they're the biggest queers in the world." Kenny looked over the balcony, gauging the distance to the ground. "Somebody ought to have killed *you.*"

"Whoa," Tim said, restraining Kenny. "No need for that."

Cory Kissell never lost his bored, snakelike smile through Kenny's diatribe. He casually took the drink out of Doan's hand (Doan was too astonished at the audacity of it to protest) and tossed that back, too. "You think you're so noble, don't you? The lone crusader against the big bad wolf of homophobia in Hollywood. You get your tits in a wringer and you shout about what a big lie it all is. Well, honey, I've got news for you: This town *is* a lie. Do you think it's just the fags, just Jeff and Jennifer Breeze marrying and adopting kids? Don't you know it's always been like this? Joan Crawford smiling with Christina for the cameras, before she hauls her inside by the ear and beats the crap out of her. Bing Crosby making happy family orange juice commercials— he used to beat the crap out of his kids, too. 'Happily married' straight guys who can't keep their peckers in their pockets, teenage porn starlets getting the studios to buy up the negatives from their first career once they make it legit, and didn't you ever hear the phrase 'I knew Doris Day before she was a virgin'? So what makes your lie so special, eh? What makes your lie the one lie that you have to crusade against, when it's all about *making lies in the first place!''* He smiled triumphantly.

"I'll tell you what makes it different," Kenny said, steel in his voice. "You wipe us out. You'll make a movie for black audiences, you'll make movies for women, you'll make movies for beer-swilling dudes. But you won't make movies for us. You won't make movies with us in them, unless we get ax murdered. And it's not as if there aren't enough of us to make it profitable, no, that's not it. Oh, you'll make a movie with a lead gay character, as long as it's played by a straight man, as long as it's Tom Hanks or Robin Williams. Or as long as it's played by a closet case like Norman Layne! So why not? Are you really afraid of what middle America will think of you? Hell, no! Bruce Willis can shout 'motherfucker' ten thousand times in one movie and his wife can make flicks where she never puts her clothes *on*, and you know the holy rollers don't like that. No, I know now what it is: *You're all fags, and you all hate yourselves, and that's why you won't let there be any gay characters or gay actors.* Well, it's not going to be like that anymore. Do you really think the next generation is going to allow itself to be shoved in the closet like you were? Things are changing in this country, and when they have finally come right, there won't be a job for a toady like you."

Cory shrugged. He unself-consciously pulled a jeweler's baggie out of his blazer and did a toot of white stuff. "Yeah, you're probably right. Things are changing. Kids these days aren't so hung up about sex as we were. And thirty years from now, it probably won't matter if an actor is straight or gay."

"It matters now," Kenny said.

"Does it, really? You weren't really mad at Jeff Breeze, were you? I mean, you don't blame him for all this." He extended a hand to include the whole wretched panorama. "He's just someone who got an opportunity and took it."

"And helped oppress other people like himself by taking it."

"You can't blame Jeff, or even Alex or any of the other big shots at this party. You're all pissed about homophobia, but did Hollywood invent it? Hell, no! It's those bumpkins out there"—he gestured grandly—"whose lives are so pathetic that they need someone to hate to make themselves feel better—that's who's manufacturing homophobia. They're the ones who'd get all in a dither if we actually started making movies that treated faggots like normal people. But you can't really lash out at *them,* can you? They don't have a face, a public image. Jeff Breeze was just your whipping boy. You know what a whipping boy is, don't you? He's the kid who gets the spanking the little prince deserves, but it's illegal to spank royalty. It's not fair, but there it is."

"Jeff Breeze could have made it better. He didn't have to live a lie, he didn't have to be loved and admired for who he wasn't, he didn't have to keep his real self a secret just in exchange for some money. And when he tried to reveal his secret, somebody killed him."

"But there will always be secrets here. This will always be a town more about image than substance. And as long as image is more important than substance, there will probably *always* be a job for a toady like me."

Kenny was fortuitously prevented from assuring his return to incarceration at that moment by the arrival of several burly security men on the balcony. "Will you gentlemen come with us, please?"

"That was fast," Doan whispered to Tim as they were escorted by firm grips through a consternated party.

"I didn't think the security guy would give the invitation to Lebedev so soon," Tim replied. "He must have asked for a description of us, and when he got the description of me, that must have been our doom."

"Poor Tim," Doan sighed, "so unwelcome everywhere you go."

"That's why I'm so fond of quiet evenings at home," Tim said and grinned.

The security men marched them outside and down the path to the gate. "What about our car?" Doan asked.

"It'll be brought to you outside," one of the goons said.

So Doan, Tim, and Kenny stood outside the gates of Lebedev's estate waiting for Tim's Alfa. "Well," Doan said brightly, "you sure know how to show a date a good time!"

"I only get thrown out of the *best* parties," Tim said roguishly.

The Alfa was delivered and the security men's grasps released the intruders. Kenny looked at Tim and Doan and said sincerely, "I'm sorry."

"For what?"

"For this." And he pulled a pair of handcuffs out of his pocket and before he could be stopped, he'd chained himself to the gate. Then, with his free hand, he pulled a cell phone from another pocket and dialed. "Okay, boys, come and get me."

"Get the bolt cutters," one of the goons said curtly.

"Here," another said darkly, "let me see what I can do about this." He hovered over Kenny menacingly, pressing a knee into the handcuffed man's crotch.

"Smile!" was all Kenny said to the goon, whose puzzled look was captured in the first camera flashes outside Lebedev's gates that evening.

"Kenny! Kenny! Look this way!" The drive was suddenly full of reporters and cameramen, both print and TV. Doan and Tim found themselves jostled off to the side by the onrush of media.

"I have a statement," Kenny began. "Are you all ready?"

"Rolling!" the TV cameramen said enthusiastically. Microphones blossomed in front of Kenny.

"You all know who I am. I'm Kenny Wells, and I'm a gay activist working to get Hollywood to treat gay men and lesbians like any other group of human beings. I came here tonight, to this party, at the house of *this gay man,* Alex Lebedev, to try and reason with the legion of closet cases inside these gates. To no avail. Yes, ladies and gentlemen, inside these gates are some of your favorite stars and personalities, every one of them a flaming faggot. These men won't come out of the closet, and they ruin the careers of the people who do, so I'm outing every one of them tonight. Take their pictures as they come out, and broadcast their faces to the world. Because when the world sees how many of its beloved stars are gay, maybe, just maybe, you'll all think twice about what you really think about homosexuals. And maybe we can all stop hiding our real selves from the cameras. Maybe we can—"

Kenny was cut off by the sharp report of a rifle shot from one of the few hillsides still daring to rise above Lebedev's estate. The dazed, blow-dried infotainment reporters stood around wondering what the noise was, but their more seasoned cameramen, many of whom had seen combat up close, scattered quickly. "Gunfire! Get down!"

The screams began in earnest then. "Oh, shit, oh, shit," Kenny cried, frantically trying to reach the cuff key he'd put in his shoe.

"Kenny!" Doan cried out before a bullet whistled off the hood of the Alfa and Tim pulled him down to safety. "They're trying to kill Kenny!"

"I don't think so," Tim said weakly.

"What do you mean?"

Another bullet smashed the driver's side window of the car. "They're aiming at *us.*"

"Are you sure?"

"Yeah, I'm sure. Can you help me get my jacket off?"

"What?" Doan asked, but seeing Tim wince in pain, he complied. "Oh my god." A dark stain was spreading over Tim's shoulder. "Oh my god."

"We have to get out of here," Tim said. "You'll have to drive."

"But I can't! I don't know how!"

"I can't move my arm," Tim said. "You're going to have to." He opened the passenger side door. "Here's the key. Start the car."

Doan scrambled over the passenger seat and into the driver's seat. "What do I do?"

"Put your foot on the left pedal and press down twice, then turn the key." The car started as a bullet smashed the driver's side mirror. Tim hauled himself in with a grunt and shut the door. "Go."

"Go?"

"Put your foot on the little pedal, hold it down till I tell you." Tim used his good hand to change gears; the car jolted forward. "Now the gas, just a little."

Doan figured the gas must be the pedal he hadn't yet put his foot on, this being the only one left. The Alfa lurched forward. "Oh, god, if they don't kill us I will!"

"Keep calm," Tim said. "Ow."

Doan looked over at Tim, whose face was contorted in pain. That did it. No hunk of junk was going to prevent him from getting the man he loved, yes, loved, to safety and medical attention. He grasped the steering wheel tightly and put more foot to the gas.

"Easy now, these are some treacherous turns."

The car quickly left the scene behind. But before the more intrepid crews could get to their vans and follow the car down the hill, a sedan zipped down the hill after Tim's Alfa.

"Not so fast," Tim said.

"You need a doctor. You're bleeding like crazy."

"Yeah," Tim said, suddenly feeling light-headed. "I wonder if it hit an artery."

"Don't even *say* that," Doan commanded. "Ow!" he cried out as headlights in his rear view mirror blinded him.

"Faster," Tim said.

"You just said slower," Doan complained before semiautomatic fire filled the trunk with lead. "Faster it is!" he shouted, flooring it.

The Hollywood Hills were not the place anyone in their right mind would choose for a driving lesson. Several mailboxes, a good number of trash cans, and more than one Armed Response sign bore the brunt of Doan's virgin experience behind the wheel. The sedan loomed behind them, its driver far more assured than Doan with the hairpin turns, each clear line of sight being the occasion for a burst of bullets. It seemed like hours of pursuit to Doan and Tim, but in reality only five minutes elapsed before they passed a private security vehicle making its rounds. In the dark it must have looked like an actual police car, because at the sight of it the sedan screeched to a halt, spun around, and started racing back up the hill.

Doan brought the Alfa to a halt with the help of someone's hedge and was immediately out, frantically waving at the security guard. "Help! Help! Call an ambulance!" The guard, who was not paid well enough to deal with much actual trouble, took one look at the bullet holes in the Alfa and radioed for just about every emergency service provided by the City and County of Los Angeles.

Doan returned to the car and opened Tim's door. "How are you doing?"

"You did great."

Doan started sobbing immediately, throwing his arms around Tim. "Ow," Tim said.

"Oh, god, I'm sorry. Oh my god, someone tried to *kill* us. I mean," he said, babbling irrationally, "I know it's a *murder* investigation, I mean, I know someone got *killed* to start or we wouldn't be in the middle of all this, but I never thought someone would try to kill *us* for trying to find who killed him—"

"I love you," Tim said. "I know that's crazy, because we've only known each other a few days, but . . . I do."

"Oh, god, I love you too! I looked at you with all that blood coming out and I just couldn't *stand* the idea of something bad happening to you. Oh my god! Binky!" He reached over Tim and started dialing from the car phone. "If they tried for us, they could be trying for her."

"Maybe. Maybe they don't know about you. Maybe they were just after me. We don't even know who *they* were yet."

"Don't flatter yourself," Doan said brusquely. "You may have been here a lot longer than we have, but I'm willing to bet we've made just as many enemies!"

Within an hour, Tim found himself with a dressed flesh wound (the bullet had done no permanent damage), a bed in the County Hospital ER, and an entourage crowded into his curtained-off area, consisting of Doan, Binky, Elise, Kenny, and Luke. Investigators from the LAPD had already been and gone, having managed to extract very little from Tim about who he thought his attackers might have been, although Tim knew perfectly well who had been behind it.

"It was Sam Braverman," he said definitively. "Acting on orders from his masters at the Church of Dollars."

"Do you think Sam is the only man in town with guns for hire?" Binky asked defensively.

"The only one who's got it out for me," Tim countered.

"I don't have it out for you, O'Neill," Sam Braverman said, pulling back the curtains and wheeling in a TV and VCR.

"God *damn* you've got a lot of nerve," Tim said almost admiringly. "No wonder O.J. got off, with you on his team."

"I'll take that as a compliment." He began to address the group as a whole. "I know what you're all thinking, and you're wrong." He looked at Binky. "Violence isn't part of my portfolio. I will admit that I've known more than I've let on, but I have certain clients who needed to be protected, and I put their interests before Jeff Breeze's murder investigation. Well, this has gone far enough. When people are getting shot, it's time to do something."

"What about Jeff Breeze?" Tim asked. "Why didn't you do anything when he got killed?"

"I did. I think Binky and Doan will agree I did everything in my power to aid their investigation."

Doan reluctantly met Tim's gaze. "Well, he *did* let us into the funeral. And he *could have* told Mary that Binky was a spy."

"And I spoke to Charlotte Kane about you, got her to agree to meet you." They all looked up, surprised. "She's a client, too."

"Isn't every closet case a client of yours?" Kenny asked bitterly.

Sam ignored him. "It's time to show you this." He plugged in the equipment and pressed Play. Everyone crowded at the head of the bed to see.

To their astonishment, the first thing they saw was Jeff Breeze, sitting in a leather armchair. The date and time were displayed in the corner.

"Hello. I'm Jeff Breeze. Being of sound mind and body, I hereby declare this my last will and testament, dated January 7, 1998."

"Oh my god!" Doan exclaimed.

"The paper will was from 1995," Elise said. "This really is his last will and testament."

"I hereby invalidate all previous wills and testaments, and renounce all claims that might be made on my estate by Ronald Piebald, The Church of Dollars, The Dollars Institute, or any other affiliated organization."

"And with that," Tim sighed, "he signed his death warrant."

"I leave to my wife, Jennifer Breeze, the sum of one dollar. I attest and swear in an attached notarized document that our relationship was never consummated, and was strictly a marriage of convenience, for which Mrs. Breeze was paid the sum of seven million dollars, as evidenced in a copy of the contract attached to the notarized document as Exhibit A."

"I *knew* it!" Kenny crowed.

"Aside from several gifts specified later herein, I hereby divide my estate in three equal parts between my children, Elise Breeze and Kevin Breeze, and my life partner, Tyler Anderson."

Sam switched off the tape.

"How long have you had this tape, where did you get it, and why haven't you turned it over to the authorities?" Luke demanded.

"A while, somewhere, and I'm turning it over now."

"What was so important in there that you had to keep it till now?" Binky asked.

Sam turned the tape back on, and they listened to Jeff Breeze continue. "If you're watching this, I'm dead, obviously. I planned on substituting another will for this one later, but if I'm dead, someone probably killed me for coming out of the closet."

"They never gave you the chance," Kenny said sadly.

"To the following people, I leave the sum of one dollar, in the hope that they too will find a way of breaking out of the closet and leading a normal life. And by a normal life, I mean one where you don't hide who you are, and who you love. I leave one dollar each to Leonard Fletcher, Bill Glaser, Helen Garrett, Norman Layne, Charlotte Kane—"

Sam shut the tape back off. He looked at Kenny. "I don't think he ever would have really wanted to hurt those people. I think he was angry, like you were, about how he had to live. He was angry thinking about getting killed for being gay, knowing that was a possibility, and he thought if he was going to go down that way, he'd take everyone else with him. Maybe he and Tyler talked about it. Maybe Tyler made a joke about doing that in his will, and Jeff took it seriously."

"So you concealed evidence that would have led right to our main suspects," Luke said angrily. "Ronald Piebald, and yourself. Piebald to keep the C of D's money, and you to keep your clients' secrets."

"I've given you the tape," Sam said flatly. "If I were involved in Jeff Breeze's murder, would I have given you that or would I have destroyed it?" Nobody had an answer to that. "I helped Binky and Doan because I hoped they could uncover Jeff's killer without having recourse to the tape, which is going to cause a lot more harm than good. But when O'Neill went and got himself shot, the game changed. Piebald knows you, O'Neill, and when he found out that you were involved with Binky and Doan in this investigation—"

"How did he find that out?" Binky asked.

"I'm not the only hired gun in town, you know." Binky couldn't help but give them all a look that said *"See!"* "Other people have their sources. By the way, I wouldn't go back to MDA if I were you. I imagine Piebald has tipped Mary off to you by now." Binky swallowed hard and said nothing.

"Thanks for cutting me out of the will, Braverman," Elise said, not really caring about the money but disliking Sam Braverman intensely right now.

Sam smiled. "I knew you'd manage without Jeff's millions."

"I need some air," Binky said. What she needed was to get away for a minute and think. Sam had lied, and lied and lied! And now her best friend had been shot at because Sam had wanted to help a bunch of closet cases remain loved by their fans for what they were not. What a waste!

Sam followed her out to the parking lot. "I guess you're mad at me."

"You *guess?*" she asked, amazed.

"I know. I don't blame you."

"No, you don't know," she said flatly. "You were willing to let Jeff Breeze's killers go free rather than jeopardize your clients' little secrets."

"I had every faith in you and Doan that you'd solve the murder, without the tape."

"And you were going to let Elise and Kevin and Tyler get screwed out of tens of millions of dollars each. You were going to let it all go to the Church of Dollars."

"The Church of Dollars would never have gotten it if you'd proven Piebald had had Jeff killed."

"And how were we supposed to prove motive without the will?"

Sam said nothing.

"That's right. Okay. Good-bye."

"That's it," Sam said fatalistically.

"That's it. Sounds like this has happened to you before."

"I'm sorry."

"Of course you are. But you'd do it all over again the same way, wouldn't you?"

Sam sighed. "You know me too well."

Binky extended her hand. "Good-bye, Sam. Thank you for the tape."

"I take it this is good-bye as in good-bye, our relationship is over. But I can still help you nail Piebald."

Binky considered. "Fine. But you'll have to go through Luke from now on."

Sam winced. "Ow. Dump me and then put me under your ex-boyfriend's thumb. I guess I deserve it."

"Yes," Binky agreed.

Binky went back in and ran into Luke. "Hi," she said sheepishly.

"Hey," he said, smiling but reserved. "So"—he cocked his head toward the exit—"is that over?"

"Yes, it's over. I misjudged him."

"Huh," he said noncommittally.

"Luke."

"Yes?"

"I'm sorry I broke up with you. I guess I panicked. You know, I guess I just thought, Do I really want this, do I really want to commit to something? What if something better came along? I don't mean—"

"I know what you mean," he cut her off gently. "If you're not ready to commit to someone, you're not ready. And we probably pushed it a little too fast."

"Well, that's the thing." She looked up into his beautiful blue eyes, so incongruous in his otherwise Mediterranean face, and gave him the look she used to use on her father when she really, *really* wanted something. "I mean, I think I am now."

"Well, then. So maybe when this is all over, we can go out on a date?"

She laughed. "Yeah, that sounds good." She sighed. "So what do we do now? I mean, about the case?"

"I've been thinking about that. We don't really have enough evidence to arrest anyone. We need to lay a trap. We need to do something that tips the hand of Piebald and whoever else may be involved. Ideally it would be at some event where we could find them all at one place at one time.''

A light went on in Binky's head. No, a *supernova exploded* in Binky's head. ''Of course,'' she said.

''What?'' Luke asked.

''The place. To find them all together. Luke, do you know what the last Monday in March is?''

''No, no idea.''

She smiled wickedly. ''For our little friends, it's Doomsday.''

TWELVE

$\mathcal{E}$very village has its fair, and every fair has its cause for snickers, whether it be the crowning of the Pickled Pig's Feet Queen or Rob Lowe dancing with Snow White, the anointing of the World's Largest Beet, or Madonna talking dirty to General Norman Schwartzkopf. The only difference between Hollywood's annual fair and that of any other town was that a billion people were tuned in to Hollywood's, mostly because the participants were much better looking than they would ever be in a fair out in the heartland (the winners of the beauty contests in the heartland having promptly packed their bags for Hollywood after collecting their crowns).

The Academy Awards are Hollywood's fair, and everybody who's anybody will be there (if they can get a ticket). The climax of a mystery demands that all possible suspects be gathered together in one room for the shocking revelation of the killer's identity, and who am I to flout convention? Our intrepid gang's plan required just such a gathering of suspects, and this was in truth the only event which could be guaranteed to produce all the suspects in one place at the same time without anybody attempting to reschedule the meeting.

It was a tangled web being woven this fine spring day. Putting all the pieces in place had not been easy. Under other circumstances, Luke would have been able to use the might of the law to persuade the Academy to allow certain people into positions that they would have otherwise never been allowed into. But the long arm of Mary Duveen and the likelihood of leaks had precluded this straightforward path. Instead, the team had been forced to turn after all to a master of manipulation and subterfuge, who could be guaranteed to keep the participation of certain people secret—in other words, Sam Braverman.

Binky couldn't stomach asking for Sam's help, and Luke was too proud to ask the man who'd almost stolen Binky from him. Tim was certainly not up to asking his long-time adversary for any favors. So it fell to Doan to make the supplicatory visit.

He had found Sam's offices in an unremarkable Wilshire Boulevard building full of tax attorneys; even the name on the building directory, Braverman Associates, gave no hint of dirty pool. Then again, in a building full of tax attorneys, perhaps Sam was the most honest man on any floor.

Doan laid out their plans to Sam in exhaustive detail, which will not be repeated here so as not to spoil the surprise. Sam listened attentively, leaning back in his chair, sometimes staring into space, but always paying attention. He had asked Doan several questions, but in the end he'd agreed to help. "I told Binky I'd do whatever it took to do this, and I meant it. I just ask that you make a copy of that tape that omits the reference to the one dollar to many of my other clients."

"That'll be public knowledge eventually anyway," Doan reminded him. "The will will be public record."

Sam smiled. "Maybe not. I may be able to arrange to have it sealed."

Doan rolled his eyes but said nothing. Sam's cooperation was essential to the plot, and if that was his condition, so be it.

As it had for those with more official roles in the pageant, the time flew by for our gang between the conception of the plan and the big day. There was so much that needed to be tended to! Not just the planning for the trap, but the same things that everyone else in Hollywood had to do: hair to be styled, outfits to be purchased, limos to be reserved (Sam's pull was invaluable here). Binky and Doan had both settled on simple sheath dresses, Binky's in white satin and Doan's in black silk.

The team assembled at Tyler's apartment at noon on the big day. Doan thought Luke and Tim looked particularly handsome in their tuxes, and Elise was adorable in her Todd Oldham. Charlotte Kane was there as well (in Jil Sander—one cannot mention a lady on Academy Awards day without also naming her designer: it's the law in Los Angeles). It seemed so incongruous to Binky to have a room full of people dressed for evening in the middle of a blazingly warm day; only Kenny was not dressed to the nines—then again, for his role today perhaps he was, in his ACT UP T-shirt, torn jeans, and black leather jacket festooned with a decade's worth of slogans.

"Now remember," Luke said, "don't try anything dangerous. We think we know who we're going to flush out here, but we may get a surprise or two. I don't think anybody will be bringing a gun to the Oscars, but you never know. Well, we've been over this again and again, so I think we all know our roles. Any questions?"

Doan raised his hand. "Are we invited to any of the parties afterwards?"

After the general laughter subsided, Charlotte offered, "You can all be guests at my house. There won't be any media, but I think by that time we'll all have had enough of that."

"Amen" was the general consensus, as they thought about just how infamous certain people were about to become.

"I wanted to be interviewed by Joan Rivers!" Doan said disappointedly.

"Did you really think we'd be going in the front door?" Binky asked.

Sam had wangled them jobs as escorts; they would be responsible for yanking yakkity stars away from the podium and toward the media room after the music swelled and cut off their endless thank you speeches. While nobody had lectured Binky, everyone had somehow seen fit to admonish Doan to keep his eyes off the stars in his custody and keep his eyes on the crowd for movement by the principals in this play.

"I *thought*," Doan said huffily, "this would be more fun."

"It's fun for the folks out there; for everyone in this town today, it's work. Including us."

"Work, work, work!" Doan complained. "That's all we do anymore."

"We solve this case, and collect these fees, we won't be working for some time, I guarantee you that."

The thought of a very long stretch of indolence soothed Doan's frazzled nerves. "Very well," he said. "I suppose this is it, isn't it?"

"Make or break," Binky agreed.

"So how are you and Doan doing?" Elise asked Tim in another part of the Dorothy Chandler Pavilion.

"Great." Tim smiled. "Doan is . . ." The writer groped for words.

"I know," she said, laughing. "He's terrific." The job Sam had wangled for them was that of sitter; in the event that somebody went to the bathroom or won an Oscar and was whisked off to the media room, their job was to race down the aisle and take their place so that no empty seats were visible on TV.

"So what's the plan when this is all over?" she asked.

"I, uh . . . well, I don't really know. I guess Doan goes back to San Francisco." Like Binky, what the future might hold had not occurred to Tim until someone else had asked for his forecast. "I think I might follow him. I mean, my next big project is this bio of Jeff Breeze, and I've done all the research, and I can do the writing anywhere. . . . Am I rationalizing?" he asked Elise.

"You're making a contingency plan," she said with a smile. "I hope they've got one if this doesn't work tonight." A thunderous drum roll cut her off.

"*Live!* From the Dorothy Chandler Pavilion! It's the Seventieth Annual Academy Awards!"

"Okay, everybody," the assistant director said, "you've all got your zones. When someone gets up, you go. Nobody is supposed to get up unless it's a commercial break, and if they do get up during the presentation, don't go down there; mark the spot and fill it at the commercial. Got it?"

"Got it," Tim said unnecessarily. He let out a whoosh and turned to Elise. "Here we go."

Doan and Binky fidgeted nervously backstage. Tyler's neighbor Oblique was putting the last touches on their hair when the drum roll began. "Omigod!" several fashion industry people screamed, clearly not ready for an event that actually began at the scheduled time.

"Girl, I saw the rehearsals for this opening number," Oblique said. "You have *got* to check this out. This one's going in the history books."

The booming voice rolled over the crowd again. "The Academy is proud to present a musical tribute to the savior of more studios than any other invention: cinematic violence!"

Doan and Binky watched in awestruck horror as the
musical number began. The responsibility for different
segments of this year's show had been handed to different major directors, each of whom would put his own
(carte blanche) stamp on it. The musical opening number
had somehow been awarded to Max Frisch, a clinically
depressed young man who had made his debut in Hollywood by sinking one of the biggest franchises in town.
Frisch had taken Emmett Stone, one of the biggest action
heroes in the world, and turned him into an existential
loner for *Body Count IV*. Stone's character, who in previous episodes of this franchise had ended the movie by
blowing up other people, ended this one by deliberately
blowing himself up. The studio was horrified by the end
product, but by this time fifty million dollars had been
sunk into the film, and there really was no way to just
shelve it. Needless to say, it bombed, and forced Me-
gaboom Studios into bankruptcy. However, the studio
rebounded by giving *Body Count V* to a more reliable
director, who had scientists create a clone of Stone's
character from tissue samples taken from bits and pieces
gathered after the explosion; Frisch went on to make
even more depressing movies, the kind that would never
produce sequels because everyone was dead at the end
of them.

Onstage, scantily clad, gun-toting girls pranced
through Vegas-like moves as scowling boys in black
body stockings opened fire on them from sniping positions above. The gunfire looked and sounded extremely
realistic, as did the gunshot wounds on the dancing girls.
A dramatic crescendo announced the arrival of a heroine,
also in black and armed to the teeth, who proceeded to
pick off the snipers with her Uzi in between moves
plainly ripped off from old Bob Fosse musicals. When
the last man was down in a pool of his own blood, she
triumphantly raised the Uzi over her head, and the stage
went black. No applause followed from an audience so

jaded they thought nothing could ever horrify them again, though obviously something just had. (Later that week, this musical number would be the cause of numerous Congressional inquiries on Hollywood violence and much thundering from rural pulpits.)

"Now," Doan declared authoritatively, "I have seen it all."

Perhaps the overall producer had been so occupied with supervising so many prima donna directors that he'd been too busy to see the irony of it, but immediately following this carnage came the presentation of the Jean Hersholt Humanitarian Award. Ebenezer Howard had spent a lifetime crusading for wholesome family entertainment, and mercifully was now much too old and doddering to have paid much attention to the slaughter that had preceded him onstage (as he always did when in Los Angeles, he had turned his hearing aid off at the first sound of gunfire). He launched into a prepared speech that caused eyes in the audience to glaze over instantly.

Each year's recipient of this award gets something nobody else gets that night, and it's not a different statue: rather, he or she is the one speaker who is not cut off after thirty seconds by the orchestra. And each year, the recipient takes advantage of this opportunity by delivering a speech that sends one billion people worldwide to the refrigerator. The audience actually in the Dorothy Chandler Pavilion has the worst of it, though, as cameras were prone to move around, catching reaction shots to the speech; one was expected to be gazing raptly at the old man while he went on and on, a feat that each year separated the real actors in the crowd from the mere pretty faces.

This year, however, there looked to be real trouble brewing. Not since John Huston's unforgettably endless speech had led to the advent of the musical version of the hook had anybody gone on for quite as long as Ebenezer. "Someone's got to do something!" Oblique cried. "He could go on all night."

Doan took decisive action. "That watch of yours," he said to Oblique. "It plays a little tune at the top of every hour, doesn't it?"

" 'Over the Rainbow,' " Oblique assented. "My favorite."

Doan snagged a cordless microphone and took the watch off Oblique's wrist. "When I give you the sign, turn the hands to the hour sign and put it next to this mike. Come on," he said to Binky, "let's get this show moving."

Doan nodded, Oblique started the tune playing into the mike, and Doan and Binky glided onstage to take Ebenezer away. At the sound of music and the sight of the escorts, the audience burst into frenzied applause in recognition of somebody's cleverness, they knew not whose.

The long-postponed commercial break came, and plenty of people made for the aisles. Tim and Elise pushed other sitters ahead of them, waiting for the right moment. When seats opened near Mary Duveen, Tim dispatched Elise; he himself took one several rows behind Ronald Piebald. Sam's voice whispered in their ears via transmitter: "You've got those seats until Charlotte's presentation; I've arranged for the previous occupants to be redirected."

"Could you hold this for me?" Elizabeth Taylor asked Tim, offering him her purse. "I don't want to tote it to the can."

"Ms. Taylor," Tim said with feeling, "after all that you've done for people with AIDS, I'd go to the bathroom for you if I could."

Elizabeth Taylor smiled. "That won't be necessary."

• • •

Finally, after seven thanks to family, three thanks to God, and two denunciations of United States foreign policy, it was time for Charlotte Kane to present the tribute to Jeff Breeze. Hollywood etiquette being what it was, it was not possible for a star of Kane's magnitude to simply walk onstage; instead, it was necessary for a rising young actress to introduce her. Many in the audience were amused to see one of Hollywood's most famous lesbians being introduced by one of its most notoriously man-hungry ingenues.

Charlotte Kane took the stage to thunderous applause. Whatever lie her personal life may have been, her professional life had been above reproach, a rare quality in the industry. And the level of her work had always been superior. She lent validation to anything she touched— even the sometimes less-than-quality career choices made by Jeff Breeze.

"Jeff Breeze," she began, "is gone from us. We thought we knew him . . . but did we? We knew what we were told, and we believed it, because we wanted to believe. But there was another side to Jeff, a side few ever saw."

Elise whispered into her collar. "Mary is fidgeting."

"What was lost to us when Jeff died wasn't just an actor, it was a man. A man of passion, of conviction, who wanted to do the right thing. And who, in the end, was denied the opportunity."

Mary was not the only one fidgeting now; Jeff's homosexuality was not the town's biggest secret, and the idea that Charlotte seemed poised on the brink of outing him post-mortem was causing many a closeted gay heart to flutter.

"Here now, another side of Jeff Breeze."

The hall went dark. "Get ready," Sam whispered.

There was no music, only the eerie tape hiss as the videotape began, showing Jeff at a desk in his attorney's office. "Hello. I'm Jeff Breeze. Being of sound mind and body, I hereby declare this my last will and testament, dated January 7, 1998.''

Piebald's gasp was audible. He was up and out of his chair in moments. ''Piebald's moving,'' Tim said into his mike.

''We have him covered,'' Sam replied.

''I hereby invalidate all previous wills and testaments, and renounce all claims that might be made on my estate by Ronald Piebald, The Church of Dollars, The Dollars Institute, or any other affiliated organization.''

''What's Mary doing?'' Binky asked.

''I think she's turned to stone,'' Elise replied.

''I leave to my wife, Jennifer Breeze, the sum of one dollar. I attest and swear in an attached notarized document that our relationship was never consummated, and was strictly a marriage of convenience, for which Mrs. Breeze was paid the sum of seven million dollars, as evidenced in a copy of the contract attached to the attached notarized document as Exhibit A.''

That was it. The hall erupted in pandemonium. All bets were off and all covers were blown. Tim saw another figure making for the exit. ''Who's covering Trask?''

''Trask?'' Sam asked. ''Shit! Binky, Doan, can you see him?''

''We're on it,'' Binky said. She and Doan raced across the stage and down the steps, running to catch up with Ted Trask.

''Aside from several gifts specified later herein, I hereby divide my estate in three equal parts between my children, Elise Breeze and Kevin Breeze, and my life partner, Tyler Anderson.'' The tape stopped there.

''He's not going to play it!'' Kenny shouted outside to nobody in particular, since he wasn't on the audio hookup. ''Braverman's not going to play the rest of the tape! Goddamn him! *Goddamn him!*''

*   *   *

People were standing around in the hall, talking, shouting, whispering into cellular phones. Mary Duveen tried frantically to corner anyone she could; nearly everybody ran away from her. "I had no idea!" she shouted. "I was hoodwinked!" Nobody believed it for a second. It reminded Elise of the last scene from *Dangerous Liaisons*, when everybody turns their back on Glenn Close. Mary's career was over.

Binky and Doan couldn't see Trask in the lobby. "The bathroom," Doan suggested. "Somewhere he could do some coke."

Sure enough, they found Trask in the men's bathroom, vomiting into the sink in between snorts of cocaine. "Ted," Binky said. So Elise had been right!

Trask started. "Oh, it's you. From Mary's office." He laughed wildly. "I guess Mary has a script for this occasion, too, huh? Something she'd like me to say to the press?"

"It's over, Ted. You're about to be arrested for the murder of Jeff Breeze."

Ted ran his fingers through his thick lush hair as he'd done so many times on film, an affectation grown into a nervous habit. "Accessory to murder, you mean."

"They may go easier on you if you tell them about Piebald," Doan suggested.

Ted laughed. "Piebald! Piebald! It wasn't his idea. He got the poison, but it was *her,* the bitch. The she-devil. She's the one who had him killed."

"Mary?" Binky asked, agape. She'd thought Mary capable of much, but murder?

"No, not Mary. Mary already made her millions off the church."

"What do you mean?" Doan said.

"Mary had a scam running with Piebald. Her clients make a tax-deductible contribution to the church, she gets a kickback. Why do you think so many of her clients are in the C of D? She practically bullies them to join."

That was "the arrangement," Binky thought. Mary hadn't killed anyone, but she'd sure as hell been in deep with those who had. "So then who's the she-devil?"

"Jennifer."

"Jennifer poisoned Jeff," she said, putting it together. "She was with him the night they had dinner at your house."

"With our special guest, Ronald Piebald. Who put the agent into my food, too, and told me about it later."

"To keep you quiet," Binky said.

"Exactly. He said if I said a peep about the plan, all he'd have to do would be to spray me with Closer and I'd be toast."

"Which is why you were so scared when you saw the bottle."

"You bet your ass I was."

"But what did Jennifer have to gain from killing Jeff if all the money went to the Church of Dollars?" Doan asked.

"A huge kickback," Ted said. "Ten million dollars, at least. Piebald was afraid to kill Jeff himself, so Jennifer offered to do it. For the right amount. After all, if the new will went into effect, the church didn't get anything and neither did Jennifer."

"How did they know about the new will?"

"They didn't. They just suspected it. Jennifer had Jeff followed everywhere, and when he made a trip to his lawyer's office—"

At that moment, the Los Angeles Police Department burst into the bathroom with their usual tact and discretion. "Everybody on the floor!" shouted one of L.A.'s trigger-happy finest, and Binky and Doan had seen enough home videos on the news to know that for once in their lives they should obey without question.

"It's all right," Luke said, disappointing the local authorities. "They're with me."

Binky did what any girl might do in the same situation: She ran to Luke and threw her arms around him. Doan sighed approvingly in the background.

"I've never been so happy to see you," she said.

"Music to my ears," Luke grinned, bending down to kiss her.

"Ahem," Doan said after a decent interval. "I think we should be looking for Jennifer Breeze right about now."

"Jennifer!" Binky shouted. "She's the one! She's the godfather. She and Piebald planned the murder. Ted admitted everything."

"Let's hope he'll admit it again downtown," Luke said.

"We told him you'd go easy on him if he squealed."

"That we will. Now let's go make a bust."

The LAPD had obeyed Luke's orders and not restrained Ronald Piebald or anyone else leaving the scene; this was not so much done out of respect to the SFPD as it was due to the fact that they knew Sam Braverman was running the show, and that crossing him could mean more danger than a wrong turn in South Central.

They had discreetly trailed Piebald, who had made a beeline to church headquarters; unfortunately nobody had thought to have them watch Jennifer Breeze, who had unobtrusively made her exit from the ceremony during the general chaos following the reading of Jeff's will.

Luke, Binky, and Doan arrived at the church discreetly along with several local boys in blue; a block away several squad cars were parked out of sight so as not to alarm Piebald. "You're not really supposed to be in on this," Luke told them.

Binky batted her eyes. "It's not the first time you've bent the rules for us."

Luke laughed. "I'm going to lose my job one of these days."

"Love later, justice now!" Doan demanded, itching to make his first bust.

"All right," Luke said. "Just stay back while we do the actual arrest."

"You got it."

Inside, they found Piebald in the main hall, at the altar. The podium had been overturned and Piebald was stuffing cash from the safe in the floor into a bag. "Freeze!" Luke said, gun out. "Ronald Piebald, you are under arrest for conspiracy to commit murder."

Piebald dropped the bag. "It wasn't me! It was—"

He was cut off by a shot from the balcony that just missed his head. "Everybody down!" Luke shouted. He turned to Binky and Doan. "Get out! Get them out of here!" The two intrepid detectives were quickly out the door of the main hall with their escort.

"The balcony is up this way," Doan said to the boys in blue. "Come on!"

"We'll handle this," they said. "You get out of here." And they dashed up the stairs, guns drawn.

"God, I wish I had a gun!" Doan moaned. "So we could *do* something and not just stand here!" He stamped his foot and spun around in a fury, which was probably why the shot from the mezzanine above just missed him.

"Shit!" Binky shouted. "Come on!" There was too much open space between themselves and the front door, so they made for the main hall again.

Luke met them at the door, Piebald in handcuffs quivering at his feet. "I told you to get out of here!"

"We tried," Binky said.

"We were pinned down by gunfire!" Doan said excitedly.

"Did you see who it was?" Luke asked.

"It was a woman," Binky said. "Blond, curly hair. And a good shot."

"Oh my god," Doan said, turning pale. "I just figured out who was shooting at me and Tim that night. And she wasn't shooting at Tim!"

Luke opened the door and shouted. "Jennifer Breeze! Drop the gun and come out with your hands up."

Piebald simpered. "She tried to kill me! So I wouldn't testify against her. It was all her idea."

"Shut up," Luke said. "Is there any way out of here from up there, besides the stairs to the balcony?"

"No. There's just the spire."

The cops came back from upstairs. "She's gone."

"We've got her trapped," Luke said. "Come on."

Luke and the officers crept slowly up the circular stairs. Each step potentially put them into Jennifer's line of fire. At the top of the spire, they found an open door and heard the sound of soft sobbing. "Jennifer," Luke said softly. "Throw the gun out here and come on out."

She laughed hysterically. "Oh, right! And then what? Have my trial all over TV for a year? Spend the rest of my life in jail? I don't even have any money to hire Johnny Cochran!" She giggled.

"It might not be prison," Luke said. "Maybe you could cop an insanity plea, end up in a nice—"

"A nice loony bin! No. I've got nothing now. No career, no money, I'm ruined. I should just . . ." She trailed off.

"I'm going to rush her," Luke said. "Otherwise she's going to—"

He was cut off by a sharp scream. He burst into the room to find it empty, the gun on the floor. He looked over the edge of the tower window to the sidewalk below. "Oh god," he said.

Doan and Binky, downstairs in the foyer, heard the

scream and then a crumpled thud that could only be one thing. "Don't go look," Binky said.

"Don't worry," Doan replied. "I don't want to know."

Luke came back down, ashen and beaten. "She jumped," he said. "She jumped."

Binky took him in her arms and stroked his hair. "It's not your fault."

"I could have—"

"You couldn't have done anything. Her life was over. She knew it. Come on. Let's get out of this place."

Several hours later, the body of Jennifer Breeze cleaned off the sidewalk and the carcass of Ronald Piebald carted off to jail, Luke and Binky stood on the sidewalk outside the padlocked church.

"Congratulations," Luke said. "Your first case, and you cracked it. And a big one, too."

"Are you proud of me?" Binky asked, smiling but unable to meet Luke's eyes.

Luke gently lifted Binky's jaw with one finger so she had to look at him. "Tremendously," he said.

"So. What do you think?"

"About what?"

"About us maybe trying again. A little slower this time."

"That sounds like a good plan. I guess that means you're coming home."

"Yes. I'm coming home."

THIRTEEN

〇⁊

Another week found Binky and Doan back in Doan's large Pacific Heights apartment, (rent paid by a former beau), shuffling through cabinets and closets.

"Oh my god," Binky said, pulling out a shimmering, new-wave Bob Mackie original. "Did you ever actually *wear* this?"

"Yes, I did," Doan admitted. "However, I ensured that the photographic record of my worst *Dynasty*-era excesses has been destroyed. Would you like it?" he asked maliciously.

"Maybe for Halloween next year I can go as Linda Evans. No, I couldn't stand to wear that hairdo of hers, even as a wig. Toss it in the box."

The dress was duly tossed into the giveaway box, which would be dumped later outside the Mother Lode bar, where its contents would provoke several knife fights.

"Trivial Pursuit! I should have known you'd have that," Binky said. "Keep or toss?"

"Toss. I bought it because I thought it would be full of trivia. Turned out to be full of *facts*. I always lost.

Oh, look, my old copies of *Andy Warhol's Interview!*
I've got to keep those. Remember how fun that used to
be? Halston interviews Liza? 'Oh Liza you're so talented.' 'Halston, do you have a line?' 'Who is that cute
chorus boy in your show? I must have him.' 'Give me
a goddamn line!' Delicious.'' Doan hoisted the magazines into the ''Keep'' box.

Yes, Doan was indeed moving out of his splendid
place, and into a more modest apartment for which he
himself would pay the rent. Binky and Doan had been
well compensated for their work this time: Kenny Wells
had landed a seven-figure book contract. Charlotte
Kane's lecture had paid off; Kenny's book was in fact
as much about the system that created and maintained
the closet as it was about the actors in that closet. It
sometimes seemed that the only ones not writing books
were Binky, Doan, and of course Sam Braverman, who
stood to lose more than he'd gain from any tell-all book.
Binky and Doan were content to let Kenny tell his story,
with themselves as secondary characters, especially as
ten percent of his seven-figure advance had been shov-
eled their way as payment for their help. Doan Mc-
Candler had lived with princes and paupers, but he had
never, ever had fifty thousand dollars in the bank before.
He, had once had ten thousand dollars, which he'd managed to spend in a week in Bermuda, but fifty thousand
dollars was a more intimidating figure: Blowing that
much money, especially now that he'd arrived at the age
of thirty, would seem even to him to be more foolish
than frivolous.

It was not any overpowering moral objection to
having his rent paid that had led Doan to decide to
move; rather, it was Tim's overpowering moral objection to Doan's having his rent paid by another man that
had clinched the deal. Now, while Tim and Doan's romance had evolved at a whirlwind pace, Doan had
learned something about affairs begun in the heat of dan-

ger from his last adventure. Tim was indeed relocating
to San Francisco to write his Jeff Breeze biography (also
for a sizable advance), but he and Doan would be main-
taining separate residences for the moment—even
though all signs pointed to their spending almost all their
time together. Doan was not to be corralled into bour-
geois domesticity so easily again.

The phone rang; Doan picked it up and pressed 9.
"It's Luke," he said.

Binky and Luke were dating again; Luke had stopped
staring at Binky in that way that made her so nervous,
and Binky had stopped thinking that pairing off with one
man would mean the end of her youth and freedom.

Doan opened the door and went back to work on his
closets. Luke knocked as a formality but didn't wait for
an invitation. "Anybody up for some news?"

Binky and Doan promptly dropped what they were
doing and removed to the living room. "Do tell," Doan
said eagerly.

"Ted Trask has cut a plea bargain. He'll plead guilty
to accessory to murder charges, in exchange for testi-
fying against Ronald Piebald. The Church of Dollars has
been shut down by the IRS; they'll be taking a good
look at the books. Oh, and Mary Duveen is being au-
dited."

Cheers rose up. "I wanted to tell you guys that you
did really good. In fact," he grinned, "your probation-
ary status has been waived. Congratulations: You're private detectives."

"Oh my god," Doan said with genuine fear. "I have
fifty thousand dollars in the bank, an office, and a real
career. I'm—I'm—I'm an adult!"

"There, there," Binky consoled him. "Just because
you're an adult doesn't mean you have to act like one."

"Whew! That's a relief."

"What's a relief?" Tim asked from the doorway,

having had the key to Doan's building from the day he'd arrived.

Doan rushed to him and hugged him. "We're official now. Isn't that great?"

"That's not all that's great." Tim grinned, holding up a FedEx envelope.

"What's that?"

"It arrived at your office. I was there using your computer until the movers show up with mine. I took the liberty of opening it." His eyes sparkled merrily.

"What? What?" Doan and Binky demanded.

"It's a letter. Let me read it to you. 'Dear Binky and Doan: We wanted to thank you so much for your help in finding Jeff's killer. Without you, all his money may very well have gone to the C of D. It's not that we needed all that money, but it's nice to know it didn't go to Mary Duveen. We know we don't owe you anything, but we all wanted to give you something to show our gratitude. Please don't forget us, and come see us soon. Your friends, the heirs to the Jeff Breeze estate, Elise Breeze, Kevin Breeze, and Tyler Anderson."

"What else is in that envelope?" Doan asked weakly. Tim handed him the check; Doan fainted, Tim catching him handily.

"Let me see," Binky said, oblivious to Doan's plight. "Oh my god." She sat down. Enclosed was a check to McCandler Van de Kamp Investigators for one million dollars.

"Pocket change from that estate, really," Tim said. "Elise's estimate of a hundred million was low by about twenty-five mil. Congratulations, you're rich."

Binky sat and stared at the check.

Doan revived quickly after Tim waved the check under his nose a few times. "Did I dream it?" he demanded.

"No, you didn't," Tim reassured him.

"There *is* a god," Doan said, passing out again.

• • •

That night the foursome celebrated with a lavish dinner and many bottles of wine, after which Luke and Tim stumbled off to do manly things in some manly bar, which neither Binky nor Doan had any interest in watching.

It was a beautiful April evening in San Francisco, one of those warm spring days that deceive you into thinking that a real summer might be coming, the way it does in other cities. "I miss the drought," Doan said. "It was so *warm* all the time during the drought. So what if you had to put a brick in your toilet?"

"You forget, we can now afford to get warm anytime we want. The first wisp of summer fog? Off to the Caribbean. The first drop of winter rain? Shall we try Tahiti?"

Doan scowled. "Tim is after me to *invest* the money," Doan said scornfully. "Money is for *spending!*" he said authoritatively.

"Even you'd have a hard time spending all that," Binky said.

At that point, they found themselves looking in the windows of Tiffany's again, as they had done before, seemingly so long ago. Nothing was being pulled from Binky's reach tonight, only being put into safekeeping until she should choose to stretch out her hand and take it.

They watched the windows being emptied in silence. Binky said, "I wrote a letter to the trustees of the estate today—I mean, my estate. I told them they could take their trust fund and shove it."

"Binky!" Doan shouted, appalled.

"Doan, I now have more money than those tight bastards were going to release to me in fifteen years. And as long as I was getting money from my family, I was obligated from time to time to listen to their criticisms of my life. Now I don't need them anymore. I cut up the last check and returned it, as a matter of fact.''

"Hmm. Well, there is something to be said for independence, or so I've heard. Are you sure about this? You could just give the money to charity.''

"Yes, but I'd still be taking it first. This way they've got nothing on me.''

"Well, I'm glad the money has made you free. I guess it's made us both free. You know, we don't really have to work anymore. I mean, if you want to quit the detective racket . . .''

Binky turned to look at him, appalled. "Quit? Quit?'' She smiled. "I'm just starting to enjoy myself.''